Sunshine

ALSO BY KIM KELLY

Sunshine

KIM KELLY

First published in 2019 by Jazz Monkey Publications

ISBN 9781922598042 (print)
ISBN 9781922598271 (ebook)

Published in Australia and New Zealand by:

Brio Books, an imprint of Booktopia Group Ltd
Unit E1, 3-29 Birnie Avenue
Lidcombe, NSW 2141, Australia

Printed and bound in Australia by SOS Print + Media Group

MIX
Paper from
responsible sources
FSC® C011217
www.fsc.org

The paper in this book is FSC® certified.
FSC® promotes environmentally responsible,
socially beneficial and economically viable
management of the world's forests.

**Proudly Printed
In Australia**

booktopia.com.au

for those who bring us together
and grow love

Along by merry Christmas time,
and ere the week is o'er
We meet and fix up quarrels that each was sorry for.
Our hearts are filled with kindness
and forgiveness sublime,
For no one knows where one may be
next merry Christmas time.

Henry Lawson, 'Along By
Merry Christmas Time', 1913

For I was hungry and you gave me food,
I was thirsty and you gave me drink,
I was a stranger and you welcomed me.

Matthew 25:35

HERE

HERE

JACK

Sunshine lay along a bend in the Darling River that curled around itself here in the shape of a finger beckoning, but not too many came this way anymore. Two empty and abandoned homesteads were all that remained either side of what had fleetingly been a village, sprung up in the 1880s heyday of the wool trade, out the back of Bourke, on the red desert's dusty edge.

Now, near forty years on, the schoolhouse was silent and lonely and doorless, a great hole in the floor where a curious young steer had wandered in out of the heat. The chapel had been swept off in the Great Flood of 1890, and the general store a few years later in the Great Trade Crash that took every last man, sheep and penny with it, looking for a job and a feed in town, or anywhere but Sunshine.

Drought set in then, and it seemed the land

would be returned to itself, to the redgum trees, their gracious limbs arcing over the slow green river, corellas gossiping in their boughs, and beneath them, in their shade, Jack Bell – who was, on this day, fishing there. Jack had been born on this riverbank, thirty years ago, in the June of 1891, or possibly the May, he couldn't tell you precisely when, as there hadn't been a priest or public official handy that day to note it down. His mother and one of her sisters had walked the five miles into town a week or so after the event to have his arrival registered with St Stephen's, Church of England, and none of them had ever bothered much with dates – never having had much of a need to.

Young Jack was christened immediately by a kindly parson, who had lately arrived from a mining town down south where worse things happened with a terrible regularity, so he didn't ask too many questions of the women. Jack's father was a wool classer from Sydney who would never name or know or care about his boy, much less his mother, who took a job with that parson's wife, washing and sweeping, to make sure her boy was fed and learned his letters. She died when Jack was fifteen, too soon and too quietly, the way the overworked poor so often do, but he was out droving by that time, bringing a mob up from Wilcannia to Wanaaring, five thousand head, and getting paid ten shillings a week plus tucker, plus clothes and boots at cost price. He was doing all right, back then. He was a happy-go-lucky kid with a grin as big as the wild western sun, back then.

Not so today. Jack wasn't wearing any smile nor any boots today. He was fishing; only fishing, waiting for a black bream or maybe a fat, juicy cod.

He'd seen men come and go from Sunshine. He'd come and gone himself, out to Broken Hill, up to Longreach, and from there all the way to Palestine with the Light Horse, the thunder and blood of the charge still ringing in his ears these three years on. And now he was home again, at last: he wasn't going anywhere else. Ever again.

He'd lately been approached with the idea of moving on.

'Jack, mate . . .' Sergeant Bill Greavy from the lock-up in Bourke had come out for a chat, just after a small pack of government survey blokes had been through, only a few months ago, sizing up the land with their theodolites, chewing on the ends of their pencils, chewing on the ends of their pipes. 'The whole lot is being parcelled up and sold off,' Jack was told. 'Citrus fruits – that's the go out here, that's the future. Oranges and lemons. Perfect Mediterranean climate, they say, and so all these acres are going to the Soldiers Settlement Plan.'

'Land for returned men, ay?' Jack had let that question hang in the air, staring at the policeman until he'd looked away, for the unspoken shame of the lot of it, for the unspoken thought, *I'm not your mate, mate*, and then he'd told him: 'I ain't bothering no one. Nor have I got any plan to.'

'You're all right.' Sergeant Greavy had nodded, but still he wouldn't meet Jack's eye. 'You'll suit yourself, I know. But I can't say who your neighbours might be.'

'Long as they behave themselves, I won't mind.' Jack had shrugged. He wasn't going to move. He wasn't going to be shoved off onto the Aboriginal station at Brewarrina; he wasn't going to be corralled there – or on any reserve, be it at Wellington or Dubbo or Pooncarie – he wasn't going to be told by some pink-arsed superintendent he was no longer a man in charge of his own life, not after all he'd endured to get back here; to get back home. He'd die here – whether they shot him today or left him alone to let nature take its course, he didn't care. There were potatoes growing on their own by the schoolhouse; old grape vines by the homestead to the south; tomatoes all through the overgrown garden – more potatoes there too, just bloomed. And fish – always fish. Yabbies in the dam to the north. He'd survive.

And Greavy had sighed. 'Well, you stay at your own risk, mate. I can't help you if things go bad.'

Jack had told him with a harder stare: 'I've taken risks a lot worse than this one.'

He had, and although the policeman hadn't served in the war himself, he knew where Jack Bell had been, he knew what Private Jack Bell had done. Everyone did, as everyone knows every such thing in any small town and its surrounds, even if no one around this one would admit it out aloud. Not that any of it mattered today. No one would give Jack Bell a flaming job, regardless of all he'd done for his King and his country. Regardless that this country was his by a right likewise unrecognised. But, in the four and a half years he'd been away, things had changed for the worse, and the worse. Now, whitefellers had every law imaginable to make a brown-skinned man do as he was told; and they had anthropology: *Science has established beyond question that the Aboriginal is the lowest form of humanity existing on the globe. Crude . . . Degenerate . . . Lacking in the intellect for invention, with the exception of the boomerang, whose engineering it is supposed the savages discovered by some accident.* So said a lecturer on 'Australian Curiosities' Jack had gone to listen to in Egypt, thinking it might be interesting.

Boomerang. Jack Bell couldn't throw a boomerang if his life depended on it. Why would he? He'd learned to shoot when he was twelve years old – and from the saddle at a gallop. He didn't have a rifle today, though. He was too worried he might use it on the wrong animal.

Only being home could keep the heartbreak contained, the incomprehensible tragedy of all that had happened. The ceaseless chatter of the corellas above; the frog song lullaby at his feet; the glimpses of a sweeter eternity in the stars at night: these brought him peace.

The vast blue spoon of the sky provided for his every need, day after day, after day.

And this day, he was determined, would be no different. A fish twitched on his line; a shingleback lizard blinked at him from a nearby rock; and the sound of bullock bells rolled into Sunshine.

SNOW

The gate still bore the name 'Copeland's Corner', burned into the top paling, greying and riven with neglect, and seeming to promise Snow McGlynn this land would never be his before he'd even set foot in the front paddock.

'Oh, mate.' Stu Egan, riding up the track beside him, tipped his hat back at the sight of the place: an impressive spread set into that northernmost finger-tip of Sunshine, wound all around by the Darling but for its southern boundary, where the remains of the tiny hamlet lay. 'It'll be a dream come true to irrigate,' Stu made his envy plain.

And Snow could only reply, 'Yep,' for that word comprised approximately half of his spoken vocabulary – the other half consisting of its opposite, *Nah*.

Stu leant across the gulf between them, and gently knocked his old friend's shoulder with a fist:

'You'll be right. Look.'

Snow flinched at the touch, but he looked ahead: the homestead sprawled above the river's edge, inside the prettiest stretch of the bend, yet though the bank was steep-cut here, all he could think was: *This'll be hell in a flood.*

Sure enough, a high-water mark could be seen on and in the house itself: a faint mud stain ran the length of the central hall, about two feet up the liner boards. Rats scurried at the intrusion: this had been their domain for almost twenty-seven years, since the previous owners, the Copelands of the careworn gate, gave in to the drought and the flood and the impatience of the bank, and upped sticks back to wherever they'd come from.

'Jeez, it's not too bad.' Stu stepped into the sitting room, the hub of the house. A kerosene lamp still hung from the ceiling, its oil chamber rusted, its glass dome covered with a thick layer of ochre dust, cobwebs trailing from its fringe of beads: a grand piece. Stu pointed up at it: 'Funny the things people leave behind, yeah?'

Snow supposed it must be broken, or otherwise unwanted for some reason: maybe it was thought to be ugly, or old-fashioned, or something that held memories of things better forgotten. A thought that only reminded Snow of —

'Here,' Stu called out from the kitchen: 'They left the range as well.'

Because it must weigh a ton. Snow followed him out, frowning, and frowning deeper again at the cast-iron cooker sitting within its bricked ingle. All very solid, he noted; this was a grand place, for sure, once.

And now it was his. The Department of Lands said so. And so did the sound of the bullocky's bells drifting in through the house on the breeze: the dray carrying his few bits of furniture, his tools, his trunk of clothes; the box of pots and pans and other household things put together for him by Mrs Egan, Stu's mum, back in Condobolin, where he was from – an age ago. Condobolin was not so different from Bourke five miles down the road: a wool town like many others, on a river. But Condobolin was two hundred and fifty miles down the road, and it needed to be; it wasn't home for Snow anymore.

Neither was this place, or maybe any place on earth. He stepped out onto the back verandah, to feel the creak of the timbers under boot as some evidence of his existence. The morning sun was suddenly warm against his chest; familiar and unfamiliar, as though he hadn't ridden up from Bourke just now with this same sun. He took off his hat and crouched to the boards, and as he hung his head his over-long fringe fell across the lashes of his left eye, reminding him that he hadn't had that haircut in town he'd meant to yesterday, reminding him of his name: Snow, for his hair, the colour of pale straw, almost white against his tanned-brown skin. His name was really Joseph, but no one had ever called him that, not even his mother.

Joey.

Snowy.

'Snow, what's got into you?' The fear in his mother's eyes followed him here. 'Snow?' He'd walked away, from her, from the family farm, from the quarrel he'd had with his brother, Bill, if it could be called a quarrel: 'Jesus, Snow, I'm not telling you what to do, I'm just making a suggestion . . .' About when to get the shearers in. It was Bill's business, Bill's farm, since passing to him as the eldest after their father's death three and a half years ago while Snow was hanging about in the ceaseless rain of Dorset, waiting for the wound in his side to close, then waiting for the war to end, then waiting, waiting, waiting for his ship home. Bill had only tried to be kind, tried to make him feel at home – make him feel *his* home. Snow hadn't lasted three and a half months there. 'I'll be off, then,' he'd said, boiling his guts with rage, with not being able to say or to think about why he felt this way. He packed up and went to the Egans, whose farm lay over the other side of town; he camped in the old shepherd's hut out there, sometimes with Stu for company, mostly alone with a rum, until Stu brought him the news of the government's request for applications for this Soldiers Settlement land up north: land where he could make his aloneness a financially viable and more or less permanent arrangement.

'Snow.' Stu crouched with him now. 'I'm only going to say this once. You'll never bring him back by grieving on and on.'

Him. There were a few thousand of them: so many that his own father's ending by heart disease, asleep in his bed, aged fifty-seven, seemed a pleasant fact by comparison. But there was only one *him* Snow really mourned. It was a mourning that had grazed the inside of every vein, and stoked the fire of his anger only more this minute, brought it shouting from every splinter at his feet.

'Yeah, I know,' Stu said beside him, at and into the silence, and it was true that he knew most of it.

Stu and Snow and —

Moz.

Mozzie.

Morris.

Ray Morris.

Ray.

Raymond.

The three of them, they'd been mates since they were little tackers, mates since primary school days. More than mates, they were three sides of the one character: Snow, always the sensible, organised one; Stu, ever smiling, ever cheerful, ever a little bit thick; and Moz, the one with the bright ideas, the darer who got things done. It'd been his idea that they join up, and they did, riding into Sydney together, almost exactly seven years ago to the day, in that spring of 1914. They were all nineteen; Stu turned twenty on the way. Delivering their letters of permission from their fathers to the infantry, and their horses with them. For Australia. For adventure. *Girls*, said Moz, as he'd looked out at the Pacific Ocean from Bondi Beach, with no idea their travels would take them first to the ragged cliffs of Turkey, where the only girls they'd meet were the nurses on the hospital ships, too busy to chat unless you were bleeding, and bleeding to some significant degree.

'There's not a day goes by that I don't miss him, too,' said Stu. 'But, mate, you can't go on like this.'

'I don't know any other way,' Snow told the red-gums out along the river, loud white birds crowding their boughs, hundreds of them.

'Got you talking.' Stu smiled, reaching into his shirt pocket for a cigarette.

And Snow smiled back him, if you could call it a smile, as he wondered if those birds would eat his orchard clean of fruit.

*

A week on and he was at the river's edge testing the water pressure of the new irrigation pump when he thought he saw a bloke watching him from a few yards off under the dappled shadows of those redgums: khaki strides rolled, a fishing pole in one hand and a good-sized fish in the other. Snow only glanced away for half a second, wiping the sweat from his forehead, but when he looked back again, the bloke was gone, if he was ever there at all.

Still, when Snow made his way up the bank and over to Stu, who was on the ladder above the tank stand, checking the pump was doing its job in filling up the reservoir, he asked him: 'You seen anyone around, fishing? Along the river?'

'Fishing?' said Stu, jumping down from the tank. 'No. But that sounds like a good idea, yeah?'

'Yeah,' said Snow, but the pair of them stood there a while yet, with the pump thumping and spluttering diesel, and as they did, Snow thought he saw three leaks in the brand-spanking shiny iron of that tank before he was satisfied they weren't real, either. He put his imaginings down to being off the rum for so long a time, and made a more certain decision never to get on it again. It was also hot: only mid-September and mid-morning, but it must have been well over eighty degrees. He turned on the tap and let the water run over the back of his neck. The river smelled of mud and metal and his own salt, and he startled as a far more real imagining flashed: of the black Belgian sky pounding red; of being trapped, breathless, in the devil's black heart. He shook it off and walked on to the house, for his rod and tackle box.

He walked past his rifle by the kitchen door: rabbits; that's what it was there for. That's what they all were, though; that's all they were: vermin. A plague. A murderous curse. Ploughed back into the earth. He wondered where Moz was, really: his bones were in Ypres, somewhere in that field of bricks and blood that had once been the village of Messines, but where was the rest of him? Where did flesh go? If we are all just worm shit in the end, then where is Moz now? In a poppy leaf? A blade of grass? Seed scattered on the wind? Where? Snow could have picked up that rifle, bit the barrel, pulled the trigger: *Ask Moz himself then – really.* But he picked up his rod and tackle box instead.

Outside, looking east off the verandah, back towards the tank and the river, he saw Stu, slouching on his left hip, lighting another cigarette, probably smiling at their job well done. Snow wouldn't kill himself while Stu was here. He wouldn't kill himself at all: they'd survived too much, not always together, but together enough. He looked out at the work they'd done just now in Sunshine, in only a week, getting the channels dug for the rows, and clearing this whole first section of gidgee stumps left by the previous owners – bastard stumps, they had best be called, those stubborn dead ends of the tall, stringy wattle scrub that grew on the clay-loam flats all across this country. Work: that was Snow McGlynn's rescuer. Work: that's why he was here. To work so hard he would forget. Eventually.

The debt helped – the two-hundred-pound development advance from the government sitting across his shoulders like a heavy pack. The deal couldn't have been fairer, with repayments all set out over forty years, but he wanted to have it paid off in half that time, or less. To achieve something. Something measurable. Something decent. To rescue himself. A few months ago, he knew nothing of citrus fruit, except that oranges were orange and lemons were yellow, and the intensity of all the learning he'd had to do gave his mind its firmest branch to cling to. He had a plan laid out, and regardless of the crop, he was a farmer, a third-generation son of a farming family – he knew how to make these kinds of plans. In this first season he would put in three acres of Washington navel oranges, and three of Eureka lemons – he had them arriving at the end of the month. Three hundred trees that had cost him just over sixty pounds, including their transport, but not including the help with the planting; and with the eighty-five pounds invested in the irrigation, that was pretty much all his savings gone. He'd be using a sliver of his advance to have a ton each of superphosphate and bone dust drilled into the rows the day after tomorrow, in preparation. Sulphate of potash, quick lime and cow manure to follow. Next year, he'd do it all again, with Valencia oranges and Lisbon lemons, and depending on his bank balance, an acre of grapefruit. Then, the season after that, he'd begin extending whatever was thriving. It would take three or four years to achieve a bankable crop of any significance, but his plan banked on five or six – to account for any failings, or any contrary plan of the weather, or the plan of those noisy birds that seemed to watch him even as they swarmed as one to roost above the river at dusk. His first good crop would wipe off at least a quarter of his debt, he reckoned, and he'd keep up with his repayments every other year with what he knew backwards and sidewards in his sleep: sheep. He was careful. He was deliberate. He did things properly. He would succeed.

And if he didn't?

He looked over his shoulder, back at the house.

He should store that rifle in his trunk, and put the lock on it.

*

The trees came on two heavy motor-trucks, off the train, pallets of them stacked three shelves high. Well-grown, strong and free of pests, he was promised, and so they were: their green leaves gleamed against the pale, warm sky.

And a little boy climbed out of the cabin of the truck nearest to see them all unloaded up the rows; a very little boy, about two or three years old.

'Don't mind the kid,' said one of the blokes who'd be helping him and Stu plant out the orchard that day, one of three, and the one that had come up with the trees by rail.

'Shouldn't someone be minding him?' Snow found enough words to say.

'He won't cause any trouble,' the bloke snapped back, barely meeting his eye. 'He's a good kid.'

Sure, thought Snow, but he was still a kid, and he didn't like the idea of one running around under their feet, while they were busy.

The boy didn't do any such thing, though. As the men set to it, easy work in the turned earth and the plots all marked out down string lines, the boy did as he was told: first, making a remarkable effort at collecting the hessian sacks the trees had travelled in, and then, when he'd tired, he contented himself digging his own patch of dirt in the slice of shade between the trucks, with a little blue-handled spade.

'Daddy, is it big enough?' he asked his father of the hole he'd made when they all stopped halfway for a smoko.

'Yes, boy, that's a good one,' his father replied, smiling broadly and somehow awkward about it, too, the smile of a man who did not care to smile at all for anyone else.

And a slight crack was rent in the dark that

Snow carried about his head like the lead casing of a shell, a silent helmet shell.

He asked the man of the boy, 'What's his name?'

'Gordie,' the man nodded, 'Gordon,' but still he didn't meet his eye, repeating: 'He's a good kid.'

Obviously, but Snow didn't ask why. The pain of it was written in the lines of the man's face; deep, grey lines, and yet he couldn't have been much older than Snow was himself, that was, at last count, twenty-six. They were lines Snow recognised, although he didn't know the man.

When he and the boy and the others were gone in their trucks, Stu said at their dust: 'That feller with the kid, his name's Ross Brock. He's had a hard time.'

'Yeah?' said Snow, as if that wasn't obvious, too.

'Yeah,' said Stu. 'He got home all right, took a good bullet at Gallipoli, went and got married, got his farm all right, down Nyngan way, then the wife died not long after the baby was born. She'd been a nurse, over there, poor girl.'

'Right.' Snow stared after those trucks, their streaks of red dust thinning, and he asked his friend, 'How do you know all that?'

'He's a shearer by trade, is Ross Brock,' said Stu. 'He come down the long paddock to our place last summer with a team. Needed the work – goes anywhere for any work, that bloke. Turns out his land is a sack of sun-dried dog shit.'

There was all kinds of hard luck, but still Snow replied: 'Doesn't seem right to be carting that kid around.'

Stu raised an eyebrow at the judgement: 'He usually leaves the kid at home – the good women of Nyngan fight for the privilege of looking after him, so I heard – but he'd been away for a few weeks straight and didn't want to leave him again so soon. That's why he brought him here, just for this short job, up and back on the train, give the kid a bit of joy. Didn't put you out, did it?'

Snow looked at Stu, as he often did, wondering: what would it be like to be the type of bloke that could get that kind of chat on others? To get others chatting like that over a smoke and a brew, be it a bottle of beer or a cup of tea. Snow had never been much of a talker, regardless of beverage; nothing to do with the war, more the way he was made. He wondered of himself: *Maybe I don't care about the troubles of other men; maybe there's always been something wrong with me.*

He had no time to think more on it; he had to get the trees watered in. Over at the tank, the valve shrieked under his grasp with newness, and the pipes rang with filling across the top of each of the fields, oranges one side and lemons the other, spilling out then into the channels all down the rows. He and Stu stood and watched the water run. The system worked just as it should, just as Snow hoped it would, worth every penny and pound. The trees seemed to grow half an inch before his eyes; he seemed to feel their roots moving through the ground, finding their place.

This is good, he told himself; convincing himself this was his place, too.

'You coming home for Christmas?' Stu asked him, because it was time for him to be heading home to Condobolin himself; he'd been almost three weeks in Sunshine, and he had to get back to his own work, his own farm, his father's farm that would be his one day; he had to get back to a girl he'd lately got sweet on, too.

'Nah,' said Snow. 'Can't leave the trees so soon for that.'

Stu gave him a look that said, *You've got to stop this*, but he only touched his fist to the blunt bony edge of Snow's shoulder: 'You have any need, send word, send a telegraph if you have to, I'll get here quick as I can.'

'Thanks, mate,' said Snow, and at first light the next morning, his mate was gone, his oldest friend, maybe his only friend, slouching over to his left even on a horse.

Snow didn't watch him too long after the wave; he went down to the pump, at the river, not for any reason other than to check it over once more. He wouldn't fill the tank again yet for another two days, such as the clock of this crop was set.

All was good. He gazed out along the sandy bank as it bent round into the sun; the river was such a green and still-seeming and smooth, it looked like a polished stone he couldn't remember the name of – his sister, Pattie, had a small statue of a cat made out of the stuff. Japanese or something. She was a kid last time he saw her, plaits swinging as she ran to kiss him farewell; she was married now, to a bloke called Sanderson, at Eugowra. Snow hadn't seen her since that day he left, his ship pulling out from Circular Quay, his mother and his sister lost in the crowd. And at that thought, he saw he hadn't got home himself, yet. Where was he, then? Where did the spirit go? Was there any such thing? Was it possible to know?

The rising sun blast gold across the water, a sudden burst, picking out the ripples that were a second ago unseen. And it was then he saw the fisherman again, looking straight back at him. Snow blinked, thinking it might have been the sun in his eyes, but this time, the man stayed where he was, under the redgum boughs, watching, making his presence felt, not twenty yards off. And in this brightening light Snow also saw the man was a blackfeller, his bare feet brown against the ash-coloured mud of the bank.

Great, that's all I need, Snow thought, *a mob of blacks camping along the river.*

He didn't have anything against blacks, not really, but they always made a mess and had their hand out, the government always looking after them, giving them rations for nothing, putting them up on reserves, all expenses paid. They made him uncomfortable, the way any and all outcasts can tend to do – like it's your fault they are the way they are. Besides, the last thing he wanted was company, of any kind.

Snow raised his hand and gestured for the blackfeller to clear off. He didn't want an argument; he didn't want a conversation. Weren't the blacks of this district meant to have been rounded up anyway? That's what he'd been told when he signed for the land. He hoped the bloke would get the message, disappear, and that would be the end of it.

But this blackfeller only stood there, giving back a little salute at the well-bashed brim of his hat, before turning away – slowly.

Smart arse, thought Snow. He'd show him the rifle next time.

GRACE

Even the flyscreen at the front door of her new home
was beautiful, so thought Grace Lovelee. The
timber frame was inset with an elegant oval window,
surrounded by a fretwork of such curling, swirling
whimsy, it made her smile to find it here, so far into
the famed Australian outback, so far from home. Not
that flyscreens were necessary at home. There weren't
so many flies in Chippenham, Wiltshire; it would be
getting cold there now, almost the end of October.
She closed her eyes and felt the sleet prickling her
face, tickling the tip of her nose; she opened them
again upon the flyscreen. The paint was flaking here
and there, but it was such a pretty blue, Grace decided
she'd try to match the colour, if she could. She looked
over her shoulder, back across the tufty field that was
her front lawn in this place, sprinkled with tiny white
flowers that had gold centres, and golden flowers that

had coppery centres, all the way down to the river, and she looked up from under the awning of the verandah: her door was the colour of this enormous, smiling sky.

Sunshine: the name of her new home smiled everywhere around her.

In the distance, off towards the tumbledown schoolhouse, she could hear her husband, Art, hammering away; he was constructing the canvas-shade colonnades for his plant nursery, nearer the water. An engineer, of the railroads and bridges sort, or so he had been; now he was going to grow things: citrus saplings, apricots, plums, grapes – the seedless ones, for sultanas – and strawberries and melons and whatever else he chose. And, while he was at it, he'd doubtless compose the odd ode or several to his adventures in horticulture. He sang whenever the mood took, making things up as he went along, and lately at the top of his lungs: 'All fruits bright and juiciful! All sweetness great and small! Seeds and blooms and nutty loons, Art Lovelee grows them all . . .'

Moods: Art knew a few of those. Grace hoped the sun was not biting him too badly out there, nearing midday as it was, but she knew better than to go all the way over to him to suggest he might take a break for lunch in the cool of indoors. Not today.

Today's mood was Obsession, as it had been more or less for the past seven days so far, and of all his moods – the most frequent others being Depression, Dancing Dawg and Naughty Boy – Obsession was his most unreasonable. She adored him – he was tall, sort of handsome and often hilarious – but he was exhausting at times; and busy exhausting himself at this time. She'd see to his sunburn this evening, if it needed her attention.

'Oranges and lemons, say the bells of Saint Clemens. Pancakes and fritters, say the bells of Saint Peter's . . .' She sang her own little fruity loop of a song as she swept the verandah of overhead cobwebs. She'd swept everything twice already – all she'd done that first week since they'd arrived was sweep and scrub and scour, the house revealing more and more of its beauty each time, in its tessellated tiles of red diamonds and black stars, its ornate cornices scallop-edged and stuffed with blooms of every kind, garlands carved into every internal door, and tinier reflections of same delicately rendered upon every porcelain handle – but almost three decades' accumulation of dust, bird-doings and dead insects would take another few rounds, at least.

For all its neglect, though, the house was in re-markable condition – nothing like the 'dilapidated dwelling' that was said to have existed here. It sat slightly higher than all else in this little nook of the Darling, so it had never been damaged by flood; the gate around its yard had been locked for all those years, too, locking out all but the slowest of slow-baking time. Paint-flaking time. Wallpaper-peeling time. The oldest continent on the globe kind of time. Grace had read everything about Australia she could find once Art declared that he was returning to Sydney and taking her with him, and she'd devoured each word, each absurd detail, with such delighted excitement – such relief. She'd thought his renewed enthusiasm for grasping the future was a sign that he was at last recovered. A sharp little laugh leapt from her at that memory – of her naivety, of how blinded she was by their lovemaking, and how *much* lovemaking they had enjoyed. She was a nurse, or had been then; she should have known he wasn't recovered. He would never recover. And that was all right. They would live life their way, as it came, and in gratitude that they had lives to be getting on with. She'd go anywhere with him or for him. She'd go to the moon.

She laughed again, at the fact of where she had actually gone – laughed at this extraordinary place. 'Back O' Bourke', they called it, joking and not joking at all, and she laughed at it both ways several times a day. Her Art was mad to have carted her off out here, he was undoubtedly mad in every way, but not bereft of logic. Mad logic, and there was beauty in that, too. When they'd arrived in Sydney, his home town, he was immediately offered a job with the Public Works Department, and almost just as immediately broke down at every loss he found on every corner of the city, and all along the train line to Stanmore, where they'd rented a small lacy-faced cottage not far from Art's parents' house: friends not returned, or not returned whole; he'd wept for hours, mutely, unreachably, at the discovery that one fellow who'd bullied him mercilessly at school had since been crippled, both legs sheared off at the knees. 'G'day, Artie, how're you going?' faces in the street would ask him, and all he wanted to do was run away; sometimes he did.

He told her: 'I can't stay here. I shake the mortar from the bricks just by my breathing.'

She understood without further explanation; it was too hard. Too painful being so outstandingly intact on the outside and so smashed on the inside; so unspeakably monstrous all over. 'Shall we go back to Wiltshire?' she'd asked him, and not only because she'd been feeling somewhat homesick amid Sydney's harsh and over-brassy clatter. Her parents were in England; her friends, too, old and new; the ease of class clarity, familiarity; in any event, she and Art had a little money of their own to fritter over indecisions, as she'd received a small but very much appreciated inheritance from an aunt just as the war had ended – and having received it at that time it seemed only too apt to fritter at least a bit of it.

But he'd told her: 'No. I want some land. A few acres. Farmland. Somewhere . . .'

'Oh?' she'd queried carefully, a little worried he might be tumbling towards very unwell once more.

But he'd winked: 'Don't call Bedlam quite yet. When I was a boy, before everything, before university, I used to spend a lot of time with my grandfather – he was a nurseryman, fruit trees and ornamentals. I want to go back there – I mean, back to that sort of purposeful contentment. I think I really just want to grow things.'

He just wanted to put things right, within himself and in the world, by growing things, trees and plants, and her love for him had grown a hundred-fold in that moment.

His parents weren't so sure. They didn't understand; couldn't. Her mother-in-law had eyed her as though somehow she – Grace – was to blame, for the changes in her son; for the war, for every fault of Empire, for every evil of foreign and faraway. Grace had ignored her; so had Art – although Grace wasn't so sure that was any sort of change.

They'd set about making his wishes come true, doing the necessary research on what, where and when. Then something a little magical happened. Grace was struck by a dreadful toothache and, the following day, at the dentist, as she'd waited, she'd picked up the latest newsletter from the Returned Soldiers League there, only for something to occupy her mind, and her eyes had fallen on the listing for the land at 'Sunshine via Bourke, on the Darling'. Her conviction that this was the place of their future had been so intense, so powerful, the listing might as well have read, *Mrs & Mrs A.W. Lovelee have lately been allocated* . . . It had seemed ideal in every way. Because Art had wanted to grow fruit, they'd straightaway looked into availabilities and opportunities in all the fruit-growing areas of New South Wales, and so she'd known that while there were nurseries in the north-western townships of Nyngan and Dubbo, there were none in the farther flung district of Bourke. One of the properties at Sunshine had to be theirs. When Art had put in his application, they'd tried not to be too hopeful – they weren't farmers, after all. All they had was a satisfactory amount of contributory capital and the verve to see it through. But then he'd won it! Oh, the thrill of that – it still made her fizz inside. What amazing luck. The terms of the government advance they were offered were more generous than whatever they might have got from any bank, and if it all went to pot, her inheritance would cover it anyway – just. Even if that did happen – even if it was all madness and nothing more – it would be money well spent. For Art's sake.

When they got here, though, just those seven short-long days ago, puttering up the track in their second-hand Humber motorcar, which, like the house, had far exceeded expectations in comfort and style, one of the first things they found on their very first walk around the property was a small vineyard gone wild – a jolly mess of grapes coming into flower. Then, further along, beyond the schoolhouse, beyond the bounds of their own land, they'd seen their neighbour's orchard all newly laid out and shining in the gilded rays of afternoon. Signs of rightness. And Art had been overrun with Obsession ever since.

He'd fall down in a heap soon, Grace knew.

And that was all right, too. She'd look after him when he did. That was the only promise that mattered.

Her broom threw a clump of some grimy thing from the top of one of the verandah rafters, and just as she was about to sweep it off the boards, she saw it was a nest. How wonderful, she thought. Birds' nests are incredible structures, intricately made – ingenious. She often imagined birds were the most blessed creatures of all: freedom, fearlessness and the ever-tuneful company of one's kind; was there anything their lives lacked?

She placed the nest back up on its rafter, and she asked again for the one thing she longed to grow. She asked God and the sun and the stars and the dust for a child.

I don't want to push this luck too far, she prayed, *but – please.*

And then she wondered about their neighbour again. His name was Joseph McGlynn – they knew that from the Soldiers Settlement fellow who helped them sort out all the paperwork. Of course this Mr McGlynn was a returned man, too, and that's all they knew. Twice now she'd walked all the way up the track to his house, almost half a mile off, and knocked on the door, to introduce herself, to say hello, but no one had answered. She wasn't sure why she found that concerning; perhaps he'd been out in his fields, or in town, or who knows? But concern her it did. She thought she'd try again tomorrow.

THERE

THERE

JACK

To the east of Sunshine, where the river dipped south, snaking lazily along from its source towards Brewarrina, Jack retired nightly to his camp, well out of sight. But he could see the lantern light of that McGlynn bloke who lived up on the corner to the north, a hazy grey-gold orb swinging out along the old falling-down wharf, right on that fingertip bend. What that feller did out there every evening, standing at the end of that wharf, was anyone's guess, but stand there he did, sometimes for a few minutes, sometimes for what seemed hours, and he'd always have his rifle with him, slung across his shoulder, its slim barrel a black scratch against the purpling sky.

No matter the time of day Jack saw him, he had that rifle with him; a .303, it was, army-standard, its long-timbered shape a relic of all Jack himself had come to reject and despise. He'd only heard the bloke use it once, though. A couple of weeks back, just as the corellas were roosting at dusk, he went out to his spot on the wharf a bit earlier than usual and fired up into the overhanging trees. Firing and firing, maybe twenty times or more. It had looked like he took out a couple of birds with the effort, but the thousand others there, uncaring, settled back onto their branches minutes later. *That ain't how you get rid of corellas*, Jack had shaken his head. They're very smart birds, so Jack knew: you have to show them you mean business, teach them where you don't want them to roost, and you don't do any of that with a random barrage. You have to be persistent, regular, get under the trees with a stockwhip, and keep cracking it until they get the message – which might take weeks. Jack thought about maybe going over to him and giving him that bit of Darling River wisdom, maybe instigating something of a peace treaty with it, but the rec- ollection of the way McGlynn had stared at him down on the bank that day – a blank and possibly violent stare, accompanied by that clear-off flick of the wrist – made Jack think the better of it. That bloke was a few teacakes short of a church fete, Jack was sure he knew that, too.

More to the point, this McGlynn had been

quick to dob him in to Greavy, the policeman having ridden out again a few days later, looking for him: 'A complaint has been received.'

'What complaint?' Jack had asked: *Here we go.*

'A complaint that tribal behaviours have been observed on the strand of the river here.'

'Tribal *behaviours*? What the bloody hell is that?' Jack had been genuinely confused at the idea; he wasn't tribal anything – all that had been smashed and bashed and outlawed long before he was born; whatever of it remained had been pushed far into the desert. 'Have whitefellers forgotten how to catch a fish and cook it on a fire?' he asked, only half joking. ''Cause that's all I'm doing here, and you know it.'

'I know it.' Greavy had looked away and told the scrub somewhere westerly: 'I warned you this would happen.' And so he had. 'McGlynn's his name,' the policeman added with a nod towards the old homestead that was now his place: 'Snow McGlynn. Tough bugger, he is, no mucking about – argued for yards and farthings with the bullocky who carted his load from the railway, no g'day or how you going to anyone in town.'

Jack had snorted at Greavy for every lack of g'day he'd ever been subjected to himself: 'Don't take it personally.'

'Mate.' Greavy had then looked at him with some pleading in his eyes. 'You can't stay here.' He'd said: 'You'll be looked after at Brewarrina, on the station.'

'I don't want to be looked after.' Jack had tried to make him hear the disgust and resentment that consumed him at the thought. 'I am a man. I look after myself. On my own land.'

'Jack, this isn't your land.' The policeman was sympathetic but necessarily a stickler for these kinds of basic legal truths.

'Shoot me, then.' Jack had thrown up his hands. There had been no challenge in his words; only a kind of equally basic surrender; an unyielding surrender: 'Shoot me like the feral pest you reckon I am.'

'I don't reckon that, Jack.' Greavy was nothing if not sincere. 'But I can't make others reckon as I do, and I don't make the law. You've got to go.'

'No.' For Jack, this was life or death.

'Righto,' said Greavy. 'Have it your way, but you should know, I'm leaving town at the end of the month, transferred down to Dubbo, got myself a promotion, and —'

'Good for you.'

'And I don't know that the new bloke will be

more or less inclined to arrest you and make you go. You know what the Super is like – enthusiastic about making his district a tidy one.'

Mongrels. Jack had turned his back then: *You're all mongrels.*

Jack looked heavenwards now into the star-speckled sky. He'd have gone anywhere to learn *tribal behaviours*, to know something of that life, to know initiation, ceremony, the meanings of the dances he'd heard talk of from the old feller drovers over the border in Queensland, to know the words they spoke when there were no whites around. That lack of knowledge, that lack of a tribe, didn't make him any less black, though, did it; couldn't change the colour of his skin, the colour of nut-brown ale; nor the yearnings that beat in his heart: for this land.

From where he sat, above the smouldering coals of his fire, he looked straight at the Seven Sisters, that cluster of bright blue stars that told him where he was, and that his mother was with him. She told him stories about these stars when he was a boy: stories of courageous women leaping into the sky; of courageous women making courageous sons, and running as far and high as they could go to get away from men who didn't deserve their attention. 'Wish

I could remember all the details as my mother taught me,' she'd say to him, words whispered at this very river's edge: 'so you can know where we come from, really.' His own mother had not been *tribal*: her mother had been a servant at the homestead of a long-gone squatter called Isiah Bell, a sheep grazier. She'd been the wife of one of Bell's black drovers, and when she was widowed, by then the mother of three little girls, she was summoned into the house. She bore that squatter five more children, and at her breast fed his white babies too, before she died, still a young woman, worn out from expending all that courage.

'Where?' he'd ask his mother, nag her, when he was small: 'Where'd all this happen? Where was the homestead? Where did you live when you were a little girl?'

But she'd only meet his questions with silence, or the sudden, no-backchat swipe: 'Be quiet.' She'd tell him sometimes hours or days later, looking into the river, at this bend or walking along the bridge back into Bourke, or gazing up at the Seven Sister stars anywhere: 'This is your home. You don't need to know much else about it, son.'

When Jack looked at these stars, he saw them all: his mother and her sisters, his grandmother, all the dark-skinned women that had made him back to some pin-prick point in time too long ago to be perceived. This was *their* land.

They had travelled with him along every road; they had travelled with him into the army – where, in his first training with the Light Horse, he was taught that this celestial wisp of Sister stars was called the Pleiades, and would be, of course, one of their significant navigational guides when riding at night. He'd asked his troop sergeant what Pleiades meant and the man had squinted at him: 'Don't know, don't care and don't ever waste my time with stupid questions like that again.' It took Jack three more goes at asking others the same – because unanswered questions had come to annoy Jack like nothing else – until finally a chat with a chaplain at camp in Egypt informed him: 'Pleiades? Well, that's an Ancient Greek name, and in that mythology means the daughter of Pleione – Pleione having had seven daughters with Atlas, the titan who holds up the world.' The chaplain had gone on about the names and stories of the stars, lost to time now, just as Jack was lost in the revelation then. He asked the chaplain: 'So, the Pleiades were seven sisters?' And the chaplain had frowned at him as if he were a bit slow in the head: 'Yes. Seven sisters.

All of them lovers and mothers of gods.' He'd learn over there, too, that in the time of the Pharaohs, the sisters were believed to be seven sacred cows that gave sustenance to the world, but no matter their names, and no matter where they appeared, they brought his mother with them; his mother had seen him through it all, and through things no mother should ever see. She'd seen him home: and he wasn't moving off this land for anyone.

Casting eyes and thoughts down at the wharf again, he saw McGlynn's lamp was gone – *good* – and an odd kind of recognition curled through a corner of Jack's mind like smoke: that he'd come here to die anyway. He'd come back here not just to remove himself from the town, and its ever-present threat of arrest; he'd come here to remove himself from all mankind, from all the earth.

In the still, cool dark of night, his melancholy solitariness settled over his shoulders in an almost comforting way. If that bloke McGlynn had his routine of rumination out on the wharf as all trace of sunlight disappeared, then this was Jack Bell's equivalent: gazing into the glittering stars, counting his loves and his losses and, inevitably at some stage every night, remembering his most recent devastation: Tricia, his wife.

At the first glimpse of remembering, she always, always came to him as the girl of seventeen she was when they'd first met at a Rockhampton buckjumping show. She was one of the main attractions – Texas Cowgirl Tricia Cortez. She stepped straight off the advertising poster and into his heart, with her long black plaits and her tasselled suede tunic and chaps; she was billed as the wild western daughter of an Apache princess and a Mexican outlaw, but she was really Patricia Curtis, an all-caste special blend of Aborigine, Chinese and a couple of indeterminate mongrels thrown in. They were both orphans by then; they were both young and beautiful; they fell into each other immediately, that spring of 1913. She was as skilled as he was in the saddle, and at any speed, over any terrain, but as an athlete she surpassed him: she could hold a headstand on the back of her horse at a canter and tumble-turn from it to the ground just about as easy as walking. She walked like a ballerina and ate like a man; he loved to run his hands across the muscles of her belly and wonder what kind of a creature she really was: she was that perfect. She was a star. His star come to earth just for him to love.

And soon enough she was pregnant, and thrilled about it, and eating like two men. By gee they were happy. He was working in the Rocky cattle yards, and the pay was poor, always a bit poorer for such a brown-skinned kid, too, and their house was a tin shack at the ragged end of town, but they were happy as a man and a woman together could ever be. He'd serenade her nightly, playing slow tunes on his harmonica from the back step, sending his love out across the sky; she'd say, after a while, 'Get in here, Jack. Come here, come to me.'

Their daughter, Mary, was born on the thirty-first of July 1914, just a week before the world lost its collective head and went to war, but all Jack could see at that time was that she was as perfect as her mother – and that suddenly he really did have another mouth to feed.

By chance, a couple of months on, as he was heading home from work, heading for his little family and worrying that his pay was just a bit too impossibly poor, he got caught up in a crowd by the sea wharves, a hundred men all gathered around a bloke on a box telling them: 'The Empire Needs You!' An army bloke, he was, in khaki uniform, a fistful of emu feathers fixed upon his hat, and he grabbed Jack by the arm as he passed and murmured in his ear: 'The Light Horse is colour blind, you know, if you're good enough. Are you good enough to serve your King?' In those days, Jack was up for just about any challenge. Was he good enough? *My oath*, he said to himself. He was as good as any man – and twice as good on the back of a horse.

And soon enough he learned that army pay was colour blind, too. He'd have to leave Tricia and Mary, but the money, so much money . . . surely it would be worth it?

'Five shillings a day?' Tricia's eyes were wide with disbelief.

'Five shillings a day plus one extra deferred and collected when I come home,' he'd told her, still disbelieving of the deal himself. At the cattle yards he'd been getting just shy of seven shillings a week and not much chance of more unless he took to droving again. Either way, he'd have to leave his little family; either way, the job would have its dangers – gored by bayonet or bull, what was the difference, really? The difference was staring at him in shillings.

He had to go.

Beneath all these considerations, there was a glimmer of hope in there that the quiet, un-der-the-counter colour blindness of the army might lead to other opportunities. As a boy, Jack had been especially keen on reading, just about anything he could get his hands on, which wasn't a great deal, as Reverend Henry, the clergyman at whose parsonage they'd lived by his mother's servitude, was as mean with his books as he was kind in every other way. Apart from the Bible, which to Jack had ever seemed a stream of gibberish, like eavesdropping on a conversation between people he didn't know and whose visions he didn't much care about, Reverend Henry gave him only a handful of old, battered volumes: from the *Processes of the Steam Engine*, to *The Sunday Book of Verse*, and the various pamphlets of *Practical Husbandry* in between, his early education had been a strange Frankenstein creation of mechanical physics, Tennyson, Shakespeare and the parasitic afflictions of sheep. Whenever Jack would ask for more, the reverend would fob him off, tell him it was best to 'marvel at the mysteries of God's Hand', meaning, he supposed, that a blackfeller should keep his intellectual curiosities in check, for they would lead nowhere.

But maybe the army would lead him somewhere – somewhere he hadn't imagined yet.

It certainly did that.

Tricia farewelled him from the wharf as he sailed first for Brisbane, handkerchief in one hand, baby Mary in the other, and that sight of them there, held deep in his heart, kept the most essential part of him alive through many a desperate night to come. He wrote letters home, every few weeks or so, and didn't worry that he never got one back except for a brief note here and there saying all was well: Tricia was illiterate, too prideful to ask for too much help and too careful with their money to waste it on a letter-writer; she was also unquestionably devoted to him and to their daughter. He never doubted, not for a moment, that she was true, that she would be there, with Mary, when he got home. They were safe and sound in the pretty little two-room cottage by the railway sheds he'd moved them into just before he left, he was sure; he could see them waving to him from the doorway. He never doubted that the four-shillings-per-day allotment from his wages was getting to her, either.

He carried these certainties with him through every sand-blown, fly-blown hour: from the beaches of Turkey to the deserts of Arabia. He carried these promises of love everlasting as a salve against the boredom — that crushing, maddening boredom — of military life in all its order and sameness and waiting, for five and a half long years, all up. He carried the imaginings of how his daughter must be growing and learning and becoming more and more perfect daily, through the terrors that punctuated his own dull days with a rareness and randomness that had him jumping at his own shadow more or less the entire time. He carried every yearning and desire for home and for love, from those first weeks of entrapment, horseless and helpless, in the trenches of Gallipoli, chucking jam-tin bombs into the nowhere that lay between Anzac and Abdul, to the breakneck assault on Beersheba that showed him what an animal he really was, the low sun glowing red on the fat white minaret of the mosque there like the devil's own beacon, the plunge of blade through flesh, the taste of another man's blood as it splashed up across his face, hot and screaming. What was it all for? Jerusalem. The visions of others he could never share. The winning of a war that wasn't his.

None of it mattered when he thought of his girls, not then.

All of it shattered when he thought of his girls now.

After his ship had docked in Brisbane, while everyone made off for that city's various pubs, getting busy spending their deferred pay, Jack had stayed on the railway platform snoozing on his kitbag, too worried he might miss that next train up to Rocky.

He made the train and once off it again, he ran for his house around by the old sheds, ran for his home like he'd never run before.

But when he got there it was only desolation that came to greet him.

'Tricia who?' A woman he didn't know answered the door, and she looked at him like he was shit under her shoes.

'Tricia Bell,' he said; he tried again: 'Tricia Curtis? And our little girl – Mary – she'll have just turned five.'

'Never heard of them.' The woman shut the door and left him standing there on the street. Fear like no other gripped him: had that Spanish flu taken them, as it had taken so many, an angry rash that had swept around the world as punishment for all their murdering sinfulness? He looked up and down the wide streets of Rockhampton: there'd been a big flood in January the year before, the January of 1918 – she'd sent him a note, which he received only a few weeks before the Armistice, some ten months on from the event, telling him the Fitzroy River here had busted its banks and come right up to the front step of the house, but she marked seven kisses under the words: *'All is well with us, my darling Jack.'* Had there been another flood? Had it carried them out to sea?

It took him almost a week to find out what had in fact happened.

'Tricia?' An old mate from the cattle yards scratched his head under his hat. 'She's gone back to the buckjumping show, last I heard. She thought you were dead – we all did.'

'She's gone back to the show? With Mary? With our girl?' Jack was incredulous – you wouldn't take a child around with you there, not with any wild west buckjumping crowd. Not unless you had to.

'Dunno, mate.' He was met with a shrug.

'Where's the show?' he asked, for there were no posters around in the town.

'Dunno. Sorry.' And that hollow, unthinking 'sorry' rang in his ears and under the soles of his feet, still yet hanging on to the hope that he might outrun this bullet.

He tracked her down, finally, four hundred miles south, where the show, having reinvented itself as the Travelling California Rodeo, had set up camp at Toowoomba, and the moment their eyes met he saw a death in hers telling him that nothing had been worth it.

'What happened? Tell me.' He shook her by the shoulder when she turned her face away from him in shame. 'Tell me – where is our girl?'

'I don't know.' She told the dust on his boots.

'What do you mean you don't know?' He was yelling at her, though she cried.

And still she could not look at him as she tried to explain, words tumbling through her tears: 'This feller, from the police, he came and took her, just about six months ago now. She was playing with the neighbours' kiddies – all the little ones, playing outside next door's, as they often would of a morning. I was hanging a sheet on the line, out back, when one of the neighbours come running around in a panic, "Mary's gone! Mary's gone!" That copper had picked her up, grabbed her, put her in a cab. I went straight to the police station, but they wouldn't tell me where they took her. I told them you'd skin them when you got home. They told me they'd had notice you were dead, and that taking Mary is all for her own good – that she's gone with the Aborigines Protection Board, gone off to school. They told me I couldn't look after her no more. They told me I had no claim against the law. They even stopped your pay coming to me, that's how dead they made you out to be.'

'What?' Jack yelled only louder at her, only more and more disbelieving, shaking her harder in his rage.

'This bloke bothering you?' One of the rodeo riders came up behind them.

'Bothering her?' Jack turned to him, letting her go as he did.

And Tricia begged him then: 'Jack, leave it. Leave it all. Please. I've let you down. I've wronged you in every way.'

He knew what she meant – that it was over between them; that she was too shocked, too broken-hearted to see him again; that she'd had to look after herself by taking up with another man – but he took a swing at the bloke anyway.

Of course, in response he got the snot thrashed out of him – by three of them – and once he could get himself walking again, he kept on walking, all the way back to Bourke, another five hundred miles south-west, trying to convince himself he'd survived worse. When he got into town, he asked for a room at the half-empty Central Australian Hotel, where he was told: 'Sorry, Jack, you can't stay here.'

Sorry.

Sorry.

Sorry.

He backtracked the five miles then to Sunshine, where he'd been camping ever since. Almost two years on, and he still couldn't work out what was actually worse: driving his bayonet through the heart of another brown-skinned man, or having his own heart ripped from his chest by the government of Queensland and kicked down the red dirt road.

It was this heavy load that dragged him towards sleep each night.

Where was his little girl now? Who would know? He'd since learned that this child-stealing business was no uncommon thing today: he'd met a few from the Brewarrina mob, a couple of escapees making their break for Sydney and freedom along the river, and a couple of others mustering the station cattle out this way, and they'd all told him there was a mission school there, on the station, a church-run boarding school, where kids from all over the place were brought, and no one from the station was allowed near them – because the kids were being taught how not to be blackfellers. Jack had taken that sixty-mile walk upriver twice now, spying, to see if she was there. But she wasn't, or not that he could see. He would know his own kid, wouldn't he? And she'd be more likely to have been put somewhere in Queensland anyway, not here in New South Wales. How many mission schools were there in Queensland, then? Where would he begin looking across that expanse of land a million miles squared? And how, when every policeman he'd pass within it would want to see him locked up one way or another?

He never blamed Tricia for it – never. Probably what had happened was that one of the neighbours had decided they didn't want a tar-touched kid playing with theirs: a complaint of some kind would have been made, and that would have been that. Nothing Tricia could have done to prevent it. If he shed a tear himself, he shed it for her.

He dreamed of her, of the impossibility of putting his little family back together again. Dreams that haunted him, tortured him, but without their sweetness he was, in every essential way, already dead. And if he ever dreamed of murder, his visions entailed wringing the neck of the one who had lied to her, telling her that dead he was, and cutting off her money, or maybe stealing that, too – so easy to manipulate anyone who can't read. Jack would dream of grabbing that fistful of emu feathers from that bastard's hat, from every Light Horse hat, and setting them aloft on the breeze.

He'd wake every morning with the dawn, with the corellas all squawking in the trees above, and somehow mornings were all right: he was reminded he was indeed bodily alive when so many others weren't. Mornings brought some remnant hope that one day, one day when his thoughts were straight enough to grasp and hold, he might even formulate a plan – strike out, demand his rights, stand up for himself as a man, bare his chest to the sun and dare it to deny him all his due.

Mornings brought him hunger, too, and this morning it brought a yen for baked potato, so he decided to sneak round to the patch that lay behind the homestead closest, bandicoot a few. He'd better help himself to more than a few, he reminded himself, since the place was now occupied, too. Though he didn't know who they were yet, he'd sensed there was something a bit out of the ordinary about that pair: the bloke working away like a slave through the heat of the day, heaving and hammering, and the woman scrubbing and sweeping the verandah in her fancy pink frock, her wavy golden hair chopped short in the fashionable way – they didn't seem like the usual farming folk of the district. They also had a gramophone, and they would play it of an afternoon, music he'd not yet come close enough to hear distinctly.

As he neared the house this morning, making his way around a thicket of gidgee and emu bush to keep himself out of sight, he heard the back wire-screen creak and close, and saw the woman step out towards the overgrown garden, basket in hand – towards his potatoes.

Bugger.

He waited, watching. She had a yellow dress on today; she looked like a streak of sunshine itself. She didn't start digging for potatoes, though; she turned and called back at the house, something that sounded like: 'Darling, if you don't eat your breakfast, I will smack your bottom.' And she laughed. Laughter that sounded like sunshine, if the sun was a woman and a posh one at that. Laughter that seemed like a song.

Then she went on her way, past the garden and out along the old track that cut cross-country to the fresh-cleared and planted fields of McGlynn. Jack followed her with his eyes, until she disappeared.

SNOW

'**G**ood morning!'
  At first he thought it was only the birds, mocking him; he'd been standing a few yards' distance from the house, planning out where he'd build his own packing shed, and imagined that those birds, so restless in their branches, were telling him with their laughing black-and-blue eyes and their cackling, honking beaks, not to get too far ahead of himself. There was a great flush of blooms all over the lemons and on a fair few of the oranges, too, but it was early days yet – the trees were far too young, and he'd have to pluck off any fruit from the oranges this year anyway, to encourage more for next.

'I say, it's Mr McGlynn, isn't it?' the voice became a woman's – *that* woman from up the road, his neighbour, who'd been around pestering before, knocking on his front door, *Hello, hello, anyone at home?* No: Snow had sat at the kitchen table, hunched over the latest edition of *The Australian Fruit Grower*, pretending he wasn't there, not that he needed to do all that much pretending; he'd stared at the back of his hands, splayed out as they were on the tabletop either side of his magazine, and willed her to go away until she did.

There was no chance of that happening this time; he'd been seen. Of course, he knew he would have to face the neighbours eventually, but even still he was scarcely prepared.

He touched the brim of his hat and began walking slowly towards her for want of any other option.

'Hello, at last. I'm Grace Lovelee.' She looked like she'd stepped off the cover of one of those women's magazines: from her white-stockinged ankles to her rosebud lips. And her dress was the colour of ripe lemons, the material slightly shimmering, crinkled in such a way that it might actually have been made from the skins of that fruit. She was such a sight, he might have asked her, *What the hell are you doing out here?* But he was too struck for a moment by the thought that she was some kind of spirit of citrus come to bless his trees.

He mumbled something that sounded near

enough to, 'Yeah, McGlynn,' and supposed he nodded in good day.

'I've brought you some bread,' she said, holding out her basket, its contents covered by a crisp white linen cloth. 'I'm no expert at baking, but it's fresh.' She winked at him then: 'Perhaps eat it sooner rather than later to avoid the possibility of breaking a tooth.'

He took the basket from her as if compelled to, under a spell, and made some attempt at, 'Thank you.' He didn't quite trust that she was real: there was a gloss to her all over, not just that garden-party get-up on her and the starched linen napkin on the bread, but something else. Besides, he'd eaten the last of his bread yesterday, and all through eating his breakfast just this morning, all through his breadless eggs and tomato sauce, he'd been battling the urge to make a trip into town for more. He didn't need to go into town, and he didn't want to go into town; he was only craving the bread: he could go without. And now here it was.

'You've put in some oranges and lemons?' she asked him, and he nodded again for the obvious, wondering how he might get out of further conversation, as she went on: 'My husband, Art, he's going to establish a nursery here, for fruit trees – all sorts. Perhaps you two should be in cahoots.'

Not likely. Snow hadn't met the man, hadn't seen him as anything but a tall, brawny bloke in a singlet hauling lengths of timber off the back of the Bradley's Hardware utility truck down by the river-side track three days ago. It wouldn't have mattered who or what his neighbour was, he wasn't interested in cahooting of any type.

Still, she went on: 'There's all manner of exciting talk in the town about Bourke becoming something of a fruit-growing centre in years to come. We've heard there's even going to be a cool store built at the rail head, so all the fruit can wait there for the best market prices. A cooperative of Far Western farmers, they hope it will be, and they're going to . . .'

She chirped on about pipe dreams Snow didn't want a bar of. Cooperatives sounded too much like trade unions to him, which sounded like Bolshevik bullshit, which reminded him that if the Russians hadn't pulled out of the war for their stupid, mag-gotty revolution, Moz might still be alive today. Snow would pack and cart his own fruit to the rail; he would bargain his own prices; and that was all a long way away.

'Doesn't it sound wonderful?' Grace Lovelee was a dream all on her own.

'Yeah.' Snow gave her another nod.

'Now, we must have you around to our place for a meal, Mr McGlynn.' This woman was relentless. 'You must meet Art. When do you think it might suit you?'

Never. 'Ah —'

'Don't be shy.'

'Not shy. Just busy.' *Just an angry, hate-filled bastard you really don't want to know.* 'Thank you for the invitation all the same, Mrs Lovelee.' *Please, leave me alone.* 'And thanks for the bread.' He began to turn away.

But her voice pulled him back as if she'd laid a hand on his shoulder. 'My pleasure, Mr McGlynn.' She raised an eyebrow at him; her eyes were grey, a soft rainy-day grey, but they held him steadily. 'Most people are too busy for dinner with friends,' she told him with that stare, one that said she was somehow used to issuing instructions, direct and straight. 'I want you to know that I'm not most people. I'm just Grace, and I'm never too busy for friends. Understood?'

He mumbled something that sounded like, 'Good of you,' and he turned his back, finally, taking two or three paces away from her, towards the verandah, placing the basket there on the boards, his breath loud in his ears. Sure that she remained, watching him, he glanced back, but she was gone: making her way down the skinny bush track that strung their fields together.

Disoriented by the intrusion, he'd forgotten what it was he'd just been doing, and he walked out into his field of lemons, none the wiser as to what he should be doing now, except that he inspected all his trees twice daily, sometimes thrice, sometimes more. He walked between the first row of trees, looking for signs of aphids or any other distress to leaf or branch: there were none. The leaves were so alive, so shiny with health and all his good care, he could almost see his face in them, see them silently working water and light through every tiny vein. Each of the trees had grown these past five weeks, an inch or two at least; not bothered in the slightest by their transplantation, all now stood hip high, and each of them was covered with clusters of pale purple buds, bursting into starry white blooms, their centres swelling here and there into small green beads, the ovaries that would grow into his fruit.

He crouched to see a hand of six – no, seven – of these beads deepening their colour, lengthening their shape. Eureka: the name of the variety came to him with a picture of all these trees soon hanging heavy with gold. All was happening as it should

– no, all was exceeding any expectation – and yet no bounty, no such picture-postcard view of plenty, could ever really be claimed by him as any sort of success. The sky pressed down upon the back of his neck, never his friend; only his judge: nothing he could ever do would make up for how he had failed.

Something disturbed the birds and they rose as a flock, a great wave, a shrieking stain against the blue and, higher, two separate clouds travelling at different speeds, one smeared and racing, the other seemingly static, confused him as he stood up from the crouch. His world spun drunkenly.

At the misted edge of his perception he saw a boy, a small, fair-haired boy, running through the rows beyond, towards the oranges – so real, he was, Snow could hear his boots squelching in the mud of the irrigation channels. *Get out of there*, he could hear his father growling across time, calling him to stop mucking about. The boy was only a memory; he knew that. The mud was only a memory; he knew that, too. It was different mud; a different river.

And yet the sound it made under foot . . .

'Jeez, Snow, look at the hole in you,' Moz had gaped down at the wound, as though he'd never seen such a thing before. The shrapnel from the mortar had sliced into Snow's side, ripping him open some six inches long and wide, exposing rib and flesh, convincing him he was going to die. As he'd never suffered much more than a graze before, he didn't know that this wound was really not all that much worse – that it would be the infection that followed which would almost kill him. He didn't know that the majority of the meat covering the front of his tunic belonged to his C.O., his lieutenant, who had borne the brunt and been obliterated.

There in the black blood mud of Flanders, on the river flat of the Lys, surrounded by the entrails and severed pieces of men and the staring eyes of their death, it was easy to be convinced that he would soon be with them. He'd felt very little pain, considering, and that had only served to convince him further.

'Leave me,' Snow had yelled back at Moz, unsure if it was in fact his friend or some wishful apparition: Moz was supposed to have been in the platoon behind his.

'Nah, mate,' Moz had yelled back, moving only closer, on his elbows.

They stayed there together for what must have been some minutes, though it had felt like hours, as machine-gun fire from both sides slashed the air all around them; three German planes swept low to strafe a British tank; two men wrestled a few yards off, so filthy, so savage, it was impossible to tell which side either of them belonged to. This battle for Messines, which last year had ended in victory for them, for the Allies, would this time end only in loss. And loss. And loss.

'Go – please,' Snow had begged him when the guns had momentarily stilled. Neither of them had any idea where Stu was by then; a crack-shot sniper, he'd been shifted off at the behest of the brass once the attack was on, and had that afternoon found his way to a casualty clearing station not a mile off; he was having a stitch put in a cut above his left eye and a splinter of metal tweezered from his cheek below it, the Canadian nurse telling him the whole while: 'Oh boy, oh boy. You don't know how lucky you are.' But for all Snow knew, Stu was dead too. He didn't want Moz to join them. 'Please – fuck off.'

But Moz had grinned. In all that, he'd grinned. That grin of his that was always keen for anything. He'd pushed himself up on his arms, raised his head to judge the distance back to their fast disintegrating line.

'We can —'

They were the last words he said before the spray of bullets tore into his face, with such a force it blew his helmet off the back of his head.

Whose bullets? Theirs or ours? In that untold mess of advancing and retreating, who would ever know?

Snow saw the face of his mate disappear in a mad red rush; he watched Moz become suspended briefly by the impact, then slump forward beside him, breathing mud, already one with the mud.

Ashes to ashes, mud to mud.

The war would be over in six months; most of their company, what was left of it, would see little action from that day until the end.

'Alive!'

Or so Snow had been declared by the stretcherless stretcher bearer who found him, dragging him by the boots through that day's version of hell; he'd blacked out somewhere along the way, and he hadn't yet woken up.

He knew it wasn't his fault, not really; oh, but how it was. If he hadn't been stunned brainless by the wounding, if he hadn't lost his head at the precise moment it was most required, he could have crawled himself back to safety. He could have crawled with Moz back to their trench line. They would have made it.

'Yaark!' A bird swooped down through the rows,

where the boy had been just a moment ago, rustling among the young branches, wings slapping.

'You bastard,' Snow spat into the mud at his feet, this rich red mud of the Darling, churned only with the flesh of hungry worms: alive.

Alive.

And he turned back to the house for his rifle.

GRACE

A small swift bird darted across her path as she reached the old vineyard at the outer bounds of her own garden, and she looked up from her concern for the neighbour, McGlynn: one bird, two – half a dozen, all dipping and scudding towards the rounded tin awning of the back verandah.

Swallows! She smiled at the sight. They were called welcome swallows, here, with their gingery faces bright against blue-black heads, and not much different from the barn swallows of her home. Such dear little things, swooshing about like cupid's arrows. *So, you've come for your nest, have you?* She smiled deeper still.

But just as much like a tiny squadron of Fliegertruppe Fokkers, the swallows doubled back, spinning around her, on reconnaissance, sizing up the enemy, and concern returned to her. Some days, or most days in some way, it seemed the war would never end. She'd seen its ceaselessness plainly just now in Joseph McGlynn's fearful, go-away eyes.

Like him, Grace had acquired a kind of second sight, and for her it came as a grey-grimy film underlaying every other more immediate reality: an X-ray showing the bones beneath all we see. She saw at this moment, her ramshackle vine trellises and the beautiful house beyond fall away to reveal the smashed-down stumps and shattered timbers of what had once been the market town of Albert on the Somme. For a sliver of a second, the old school-house in the distance, closer to the river, seemed to be smoking, but it was only the heat haze. She blinked it away. She snatched all thought away from that place.

'Darling!' she called out to Art as she reached the back step.

He didn't answer; she didn't really expect him to: he was crashing. She took a deep breath, sent the usual prayer out along the warm breeze, supposing he might have slunk back off to bed. When she'd left him, half an hour or so ago, with a small pile of honey-buttered toast and tea, she knew more or less where he was heading. Uncanny, the way the body gave up something of the mind's secrets before a word was spoken: the muscles in his face would always go first, as though he were melting. 'What are you thinking?' she used to ask him when she saw this sign, and he would say: 'Nothing. That's the problem – it's nothing. I feel nothing. I am nothing.'

He was suffering from some residual and persistent disorganisation of the brain – obviously. Still, he'd come a long way since she'd first met him, at The Special, in Surrey – the convalescent hospital dedicated to the deranged. Officers only. He could barely move at all; curious case of nervous paralysis. Three days' solid shelling at Pozieres, that'd do it to you – and he'd been like that for over four months by the time she arrived that December of 1916, a kind of casualty herself, having been shipped back to Blighty after a series of fainting spells brought on by exhaustion. It wasn't uncommon among the nurses – it was nonstop horror and there was either never quite enough to eat or no appetite for it – but it had been embarrassing to have suffered such a sidelining, such a dismissal. Not as embarrassing as the condition of Captain Arthur Lovelee, though. She'd recognised his frustration and humiliation right away: lying there on a cloud featherdown beneath a pretty bay window in what had lately been Lord Whatshisname's drawing room. Goodness gracious: she'd been informed that this Captain Lovelee had been recommended for some sort of above-and-beyond gallantry in the field, some breakneck Australian brutality that had shocked even Fritz, and here he was tucked into bed like a baby.

His eyes, blue in every sense, begged her as she neared: *HELP ME*.

The standard treatment then was to pretend none of it was happening. Can't move your legs? Can't feed yourself? Never mind. We'll have a singalong this afternoon, 'Let Me Call You Sweetheart,' have another spoonful of jelly and custard so you can feel sick in the stomach too. These men weren't children; quite the opposite. Grace knew all too well: as surgical nurse and do-it-yourself butcher when circumstances required, she'd too often been up to her elbows in the very substance of them. Cured her of any desire to make medicine a profession; cured her of any desire to bother much about anything at all, at that time.

'Oh dear me, shit soup for tea,' were the first words she'd said to Art Lovelee, spooning cauliflower mush at him as if he'd lost his teeth. His teeth were strong and straight and white and shame was their shared currency.

And he spat the mush all down the front of her pinny.

'Oh flick it, I'm so sorry!' She leapt to tidy up the slop, and to apologise, sincerely. 'I'm so terribly sorry, sir.' She'd supposed, being Australian, he'd find the vulgarity a little cheering; she'd only hoped to ease his suffering. In her experience, an Australian might have half an arm off, hanging by its sinews, and feel the need to make a grim quip about it.

'S-s-s'all right,' this one stammered, it having taken him a good minute to get the words out. 'L-l-laughing,' he added, and right there she saw it was true – he was laughing. She saw the light of it sparkling in his eyes, and something sparked between them in that moment: a friendship firm and forever.

'He hasn't said a word since being brought in,' one of the doctors told her later that day. 'He didn't buckle in the line, you know – collapsed only in pulling out, finding most of his company gone. Been a mystery to us ever since. Whatever you're doing, nurse, keep at it.'

So she did; she sat with him every day, for however long her duties allowed, and little by little over that first fortnight, with lots of very bad jokes, she coaxed his words out, she laughed his stammer away. They never talked about what happened on the Somme; they probably never would; she was no more inclined to share her own memories of the front. She didn't mention his paralysis, either. No one seemed to know where to begin with that: a big, strapping man, one moment leading in the field, the next, helpless. Every test had been tried: there was nothing wrong with him physically, no sensory damage, no rupture of the spine. When a doctor had jabbed a pin into his toe, he cried, 'Ouch!' and flinched, but when asked to wriggle it – no show. She tried a few tricks instead: dropping a plate; pretending to slip; exclaiming, 'Oh look!' at the snow falling outside the windows behind him. But he remained unmoving.

And then, just as she thought his condition was too complex for words, or her words at least, he surprised her again. On Christmas morning, as she brought in his festive fruit bun and marmalade, she teased, 'Ah but have you been a good boy?' and he teased back, 'Never – the things I do when you're not looking.' Her heart burst for his predicament, for the whole, wide ocean of not-secret secrets that stretched between them and washed them together at once. She put the tray on the nightstand and sat beside him on the bed; break one rule, break the next: she took his hand in hers and squeezed an assurance: 'I have no doubt whatsoever that you get up to all manner of nonsense.'

At which he nodded, and his eyes filled with tears.

'Well done, me.' She squeezed his hand again: 'Now I've upset you.'

'No.' He smiled and shook his head; he glanced down at his hand in hers: 'It's just that . . . Well . . . I haven't been touched with any affection, like this, for quite some time.'

What creature is man that one in such deep grief, in such need of having his hand held, had not had that simple need met? She felt the revelation rise inside her and with it her own tears. She kept hold of his hand; she poured all the strength of her affection and respect into this touch, and his tears streamed as she did, blotting into the soft blue flannel of his pyjama shirt.

'What a display I'm putting on.' He sniffed. 'Christmas display. Just for you. You must think I'm a pathetic heap.'

'No,' she said. She wanted to wipe the tears from his face, but she didn't want to let go of his hand, and she didn't want to take his tears away from him now that they were here: they were dignified tears.

'I would never think less of a man for expressing what is necessary.'

She squeezed his hand once more, with the promise of her words; and then – to the amazement of them both – he squeezed her hand back.

Before the end of January, he was up and out of bed, and asking her to the pictures.

By midsummer, they were planning their wedding: modest and quick, as war weddings almost invariably are, and in her home parish at Chippenham.

'He's not right in the head,' her mother had said in warning, not unkind about it; only stating a patent truth. He'd been honourably discharged from the army and shoe-horned into a consulting engineer's job overseeing the final plumbing details of Australia House, the new High Commission building in London, but he was only just coping: beneath the easy Aussie banter he was dithery, always slightly dishevelled and often hard-pressed to tell you what day of the week it was; prone to dancing, especially with his new mother-in-law, reciting tracts of some antipodean poet no one had ever heard of, and drinking vast quantities of beer – often all at the same time.

'Fine fellow!' her father bellowed merrily

whenever they visited. As branch manager of the local Capital and Counties Bank and amateur railways enthusiast, he was delighted to have a real engineer in the family, and a soldier at that, however broken. 'What will you drink – bitter or stout?'

By the following Christmas, though, when the sky set in all shit-soup grey and the streets were slick with ice, Art was sent off to inspect some of the structural damage caused by a Zeppelin bombing raid over central London, and on returning to their Hammersmith flat, he said: 'I'm very tired, my love. Very tired.' It was about half-past four in the afternoon, and night had fallen; he went to bed, and stayed there for almost three weeks. Melting.

All she could do was have a message sent up to his office, apologising, lying – *dreadful winter chest cold* – and then join him in bed.

Where she asked him: 'What do you want, darling?'

'I want the war to end.'

Didn't they all. Since she couldn't give him that, she loved him and held him, and held him and loved him, until he roused, until he rallied, until he said:

'I want to give you more than this, my love, my wonder. I want to give you the sun. *My* sun. I want to go home. Let's go home – to Australia.'

And here they were.

'Darling!' she called out to him again, in the here and the now. The back flyscreen slapping shut behind her, she noted the toast untouched on the bench by the sink, a trail of ants making their way up the leg nearest; a blowfly buzzing about, having followed her in. She allowed herself to feel the stab of resentment: *Oh God, not again.* At least he wasn't a nasty drunk, she told herself. At least he wasn't cruel – not ever. But how she despised this phase; this shade: Depression. She wanted to lock the door on him, not see him until it passed. Not see his face. And the thought of not seeing his face again quickened her step down the hall.

'Art, darling. Darling Art,' she lightened her voice in the cool, dark heart of this house. A beat of fear, of nightmares that shook her more than any other: that one day, he'd break the pattern of his fracturing and she'd never find him in any condition again, other than gone.

But here he was, just where she supposed he'd be: lying on the tangled mess of sheets, in singlet and undershorts, long legs stretched out, crossed at the ankles, notebook open facedown over his thigh. He could be any chap spending a morning at leisure. Any chap who'd lost the ability to smile. A chap on the desert's edge in every sense.

She said: 'Hm. Well. Well. We know what's going to happen now, don't we.'

'We do.' He nodded. 'That McGlynn a more miserable sod than me?'

'Oh heavens, yes,' she said, reaching behind her to unbutton her dress. 'Twice as miserable and ten times more soddish. Better looking, though.'

Art snorted: 'Not hard.'

Perhaps not, she smiled to herself. There were many more handsome men – oh but how she loved this one. Why? Call it a survival pact; a safety pact: he pulled her away from darker paths, too, mostly by keeping her so busy.

'What have you been scribbling?' she asked him, hanging up her dress.

'Trying to remember why I'm doing this.' He tossed the book on the bedside table. 'Why I'm here. How I'm going to keep so many young plants alive, and why I should attempt it.'

Oh dear God – no. He hadn't even constructed the seedbeds yet, nor seen the rootstock ordered up from Nyngan for the citrus, and already he was fretting that he would kill them. Perhaps this business of growing things wasn't such a good idea. How would he cope if they *did* all die? And how could she help prevent any such disaster occurring? She wasn't a farmer. She'd never grown anything more than a potted geranium on a windowsill: that blackened and gave up after the first heavy frost. Highly unlikely there'd be a frost here; highly unlikely the river would run dry. This was the perfect place for growing things. Wasn't it? She shoved her panic down, deep as it would go, and dropped her slip and her knickers to the floor.

She told him: 'You're making a future for us. From us.' *Please*, she glanced over her shoulder at the sky outside their bedroom window: *Please, bring us a child.*

'It's been almost four years,' he said. 'Perhaps God is being kind by denying us.'

No. 'God has far too much on his mind. I, on the other hand . . .'

'I'm tired, Grace.' He tried so very hard to smile, to put her off, to make her leave him alone.

No. 'I need you.' She did: she needed his touch as much as she needed to give her own to him. She needed to feel his life inside her. She also knew he was indeed tired: after slogging away like an actual lunatic these past several days, he was no doubt muscle weary and sore. But if she timed things well, she knew she could turn him around with this love, she could hold him in the present for just long enough to give his mind the rest it needed more than anything else. She would cure whatever was preventing their child, too: her periods had been haphazard since the first casualty rush of the Somme: brutal one month and barely there the next; she would settle that here with all else. 'Please.'

She held his face in her hands, she held his gaze until she found a glint there in his eyes; and then she kissed him. She kissed him and kissed him until he kissed her in return.

*

The room was midday-warm, gently roasting, when she woke in his arms, and there was no smile like it. Art was so deeply asleep, he didn't stir in the slightest as she rose. She'd won this round.

It was this kind of sleep, dreamless and worlds away, that healed the mind – she was sure of it. Different kinds of sleep were attached to each of his selves: under Obsession, he'd sleep fitfully for only three or four hours, and become racked with untold visions and relivings; under Dancing Dawg, he'd invariably sleep the foggy and never quite satisfying sleep of the inebriated; under Naughty Boy, he'd wake several times in the night desperate to make love again or eat – usually both; and under Depression, he'd appear to oversleep but not quite sleep at all, whimpering softly inside it now and again, breaking and breaking her heart. But this sleep here – *this* was sleep. Ordinary sleep. This was where his cure lay, if ever it would be found. It assured them both a respite, anyway, for however long the peace would last: perhaps a week, perhaps a month or even two.

She dressed again, counting around all blessings, all miracles, and grateful for every damn one. This sleep ironed the lines from his face, rolling back time to some sweet boyish place, before war and duty, a place in which, if time were ever fair, they might have met. He'd been wanting to leave for England, as it was, and as was commonly done; he'd been seeking a position with a firm or a post-graduate scholarship, whichever came first, when the battle bells tolled – making him believe he'd get his passage over for free, doing his bit in between. If time had taken a different track, perhaps they might have met in the foyer at Drury Lane, on one of her trips down to London, to the theatre, with her parents, when she was just Miss Myles, never Nurse; he'd have been down from Cambridge; her father would have accosted him over some incidental chat about diesel locomotion, after which they'd have gone on to share supper. And perhaps she'd have found him deadly boring and arrogant, altogether undesirable; with her parents imploring her: *Time is ticking on, Gracie – you're almost twenty-two. And he's such a nice man.*

A nice man who instead not only lost most of his men on that deadly ridge at Pozieres, but who tore into the bodies of their young German counterparts during the most vicious hand-to-hand combat imaginable. Unimaginable. Up to his elbows in Germans. He didn't know she knew, but indeed she knew. When he collapsed in London that winter of 1917, after his discharge, she made an effort to find out a little more detail on what had happened there. One thing to shoot a man, or blow him to bits with a shell; quite another to slit his throat. It was not courage that earned him the medal he later refused to receive, but the worst and most desperate of fears.

How she wished she could kiss it all away. She'd certainly spend the rest of her life trying to.

As if time found the thought amusing, the swallows outside burst into song – a sound almost insanely cheerful. She couldn't tell if it was only a figment, but she was sure the laughter of these Australian swallows was louder and more uproarious than those of England. Most definitely their high, throaty chatter here included now and again a particularly long, burbling gurgle that sounded very much like one of them had given themselves over completely to a fit of the giggles.

They seemed to have gathered at the front verandah, and she stepped out there to investigate, to enjoy their bright busyness, and as she opened the flyscreen, one flew so close she might have touched it, had any human reflex been so quick.

Ha! So, it *was* their nest up there on the rafter. She supposed they were shouting now: 'It's her! It's her! The one with the broom. Defend the eggs! Defend the eggs!' She wondered how many eggs were up there, being so valiantly and furiously protected by what must have been a dozen birds; she wondered at such breakneck bonds of family – how she wanted such bonds for herself.

She held her hand to her belly, there under the darting, shrieking swallows, willing Art's life to join with hers. Perhaps it wasn't the most ideal time to bring a child into the world – a world too wounded in every way. A crippled world, a mangled world, a world that would never, ever be the same. But looking out across this bloom-strewn field towards the river, this world seemed nothing less than perfect.

A world of birds: the corellas sat like fat, white orchids dotting the broad canopies of the eucalypt trees; and among the wild daisies, blue fairy wrens hopped about, pecking for seed; a wagtail fanned its glossy black feathers from its lookout on the bonnet of the car, and – what? What was *that* bird? A green parakeet with a teal-splashed face and gold breast, a flash of crimson at its back. She blinked, but it remained – and there were four of them, foraging in the long grass by the gatepost.

This was a perfect place. She kept her hand pressed to her belly. A perfect place to grow things. All things.

A little warm, perhaps, she laughed to herself as she moved across to the far end of the verandah for her broom. She had no intention of using it in this heat – what was it going to be like in *summer*? – but it had fallen over and made itself a tripping hazard.

'Don't worry,' she told the swallows whizzing about her head in warning. 'I'm only going to put it away.'

She glimpsed the nest up there: bowl-shaped, a little larger than her own hand, and the nursery rhyme slipped into her mind with all her wishes: 'Oranges and lemons, say the bells of Saint Clemens,' she sang it aloud, half just to join the birds: 'Pancakes and fritters, say the bells of Saint Peter's. Two sticks and an apple, say the bells of Whitechapel. Old Father —'

She stopped at sensing she was not alone.

A tall, grey-brown shape moved through a copse of low bushes midway between the house and the river, about twenty yards off. She thought at first it might be a kangaroo, and as much as she'd been told by all and sundry what pests they were to farmers, she hadn't yet seen one except at Sydney's Taronga Park Zoo, and she very much wanted to meet one where it was supposed to be.

'Hello there!' she called out, as if a kangaroo might answer her, and she laughed at herself then, muttering, 'Who's mentally disordered?' just as she saw it wasn't a kangaroo at all, but a man.

She stood there, broom in hand, as he stepped out from the bushes.

A brown-skinned man in grey shirt and khaki trousers; broad shoulders and a wave of thick black hair brushed back from his face. He looked like an Indian soldier she'd once treated for a bullet gash to the wrist, behind the lines at Neuve Chapelle. She blinked again, but the man remained.

SEED

SEED

JACK

'Hello!' The woman waved again, setting the broom against the verandah post beside her and then she took the few steps down to the ground towards him.

Jack couldn't think what to say as she approached. She was, hands down, a looker, but she had a different dress on now, a light green one, and the buttons that ran down the front were done up crooked; her hair could have done with a bit of a comb, too. He had an odd desire to tidy her up.

'Grace Lovelee,' she said, and as her smile widened she only got sweeter to look at.

Lovely, thought Jack. *Plus some.* And that only had him more dumbstruck, supposing a thousand blokes and more before him had had exactly the same thought.

'Are you a neighbour, too?' she asked, in a way

that suggested the idea wasn't objectionable.

'Ah . . .' He eventually found the word: 'Yeah.'

She waited a moment – waiting for him to introduce himself, he supposed, but for that moment he couldn't quite locate his name.

'Where's your place, then?' she chirped on, regardless, as though his place might have been a cattle kingdom up the road.

My word, thought Jack: *You really are a posh little dolly, aren't you.* She sounded like one of those Red Cross ladies he'd met in Egypt, handing out comfort parcels in Port Said, plucked from some clipped-lawn afternoon tea, ever smiling, ever kind, seemingly not seeing the filth in the streets, the sand and the flies. An English lady, from that country he had never set foot on and never would, but that had robbed him of his own and his family – he could see that all too well these days. God save the King – for he is a liar and a thief. Jack told the woman, chucking his chin at the rise of the riverbank, where the redgums sprawled thickly over the silty strand: 'I live down there.'

Because this is my land. All of it.

'Oh?' She only grinned at that idea: 'We're quite close neighbours, then!' And she laughed – that laughter drenching all in sunshine.

Who are you, really? Jack felt a shiver of deeper recognition he didn't know what to do with. He thought he'd better make sure he hadn't fallen asleep by the river just now, and so he asked her: 'You don't mind? Me being a close neighbour?'

'Why should I mind?' She frowned above that sunny smile. 'Are you someone I shouldn't care to know?'

He frowned back at her: she couldn't be real.

Her frown grew cold; the smile vanished: 'Oh. I see. Of course. Well.' She waved her hand, dismissive: 'If we're going to be neighbours, you should know I've had it demonstrated to me too often that our blood is all the one colour.' She glanced down at his old khakis: 'With whom did you serve?'

'Light Horse,' he said, barely, and not only because he felt the first wisps of friendship curling around and through his ribs, but because he now remembered his pockets were full of potatoes he'd just pinched from her garden – second batch, too, as there were lots of them, juicy and new.

She nodded: 'It appears we're all of one blood in this respect as well. I nursed at the front in northern France and Belgium for almost two years.' She waved her hand again, not quite dismissing the pain that flashed in her eyes before she added: 'Wherever it is we've been, if we're going to be neighbours now, best tell me your name, hm?'

'Jack,' he said, in her thrall; she made him large and small at once; a gawky boy: 'Jack Bell.'

Her smile returned, so wide and bright: 'Pleased to meet you, Mr Bell.'

'Jack,' he said quickly, suddenly confused by some emotion he couldn't name.

'As you must call me Grace,' she said.

But he couldn't meet her eye now; he looked down, at the odd lumps made by the potatoes in his pockets; at his bare feet; at the fraying edges of his trouser cuffs. He wasn't ashamed of his poverty: he'd always been poor to some degree; he was shocked by the appearance of himself, the fact of himself, as if looking in the mirror for the first time in a long time – though he couldn't have said when last he'd done that.

I shouldn't be here, loafing about on the river – I should be fighting. Fighting for what is mine. The thought swept into him and swept out – a tide he couldn't quite catch.

'My goodness, have I upset you, too?' she said. 'I seem to excel at putting off the neighbours. Whatever clumsy thing I've said, I'm terribly sorry for it.'

'What?' He looked up. 'Don't you be sorry, Miss – it's . . . Ah —'

'Grace – please. Please, Jack. I'm not anyone's *Miss*. I just hope I haven't got things off to a bad start. Have I?'

'No, you haven't.' Seventeen different kinds of strangeness made him laugh: 'I'm the one who should be apologising – I've been sneaking about, helping myself to potatoes from your yard.'

The frown came quick again and colder: 'No,' she shook her head: 'No, no, no.'

Oh shit, he began to dread whatever he might have started here now.

'You will not do that,' she said, just about growling it at him. 'You will not sneak about. You will help yourself whenever you like – and be welcome to join us for a meal whenever you like, too. I know Art – my husband – he'd enjoy the company. We don't have any chums around here yet, you see – be our first?'

'Ah —' Jack could hardly keep up.

'Never mind.' Grace Lovelee rolled her eyes and appeared to tsk at herself: 'I can be a little overbearing at times. Do what suits you, Jack. Please, do. I say, though, the vegetable plot is a bamboozling load of where-to-begins, isn't it? And I'm not much of a gardener. In fact, I'm not a gardener at all. I'm not entirely convinced plants like me, actually. If you know anything about gardening, you could always help me with that, if it ever suited you. I'd be very grateful.'

So would I. Jack nodded. He'd never been a gardener himself but he knew enough to be useful: he'd often been called upon to help Mrs Henry, the Reverend's wife, in their yard when he was a boy. 'That'd suit all right,' he told Grace Lovelee. 'Thank you.'

It wasn't a job she was offering. It was something better than that.

It was something good.

*

'You might not want to pull those out,' Jack said as they bent to the work of clearing the garden of weeds and sorting out what was what. 'They're tomato seedlings,' he told her.

'Really?' She stood up with her hands on her hips, regarding the little sprouts that had happily sprung up under a shady thatch of old withered grape vines and blackberry vines and rusty fencing wire. 'Which ones?' She peered straight down at them.

'These.' He crouched and lifted one of the fine, velvety leaves with the palm of his hand. 'They sow themselves, don't need much looking after but a bit of water if there's been no rain. Sweet and tasty, they are, too. Look here,' he said: 'See these little yellow flowers?' He reached across to another more mature plant and turned a cluster of its tiny, wax-papery blooms towards her. 'You'll get a fruit round about the size of a plum on this by Christmas.'

'*Really,*' she gave him that wide, wide smile again. 'That's amazing. So very amazing, isn't it, the way things just – *grow*.' She gazed off into the distance then, a long way away.

He wondered what she was looking at, in her mind, where she'd gone; he wondered too, why it was so annoying to him that her buttons were still done up wrong: there were a dozen or so of them, from her lace collar down to her belt, small shell disks that kept catching the sun, and the second one from the top had been missed, making the bodice skewiff. Why should he care about such a thing? That dress was probably worth more than his life; she could wear it however she pleased. Still, the missed button had got into his head, and there become like an itch under a bandage: you can only ignore it for so long before you crack.

'Ah – Miss. Um – Grace?' He wasn't sure whether to stay crouching or stand – or why she made him feel like a boy unable to form whole thoughts.

'Hm?' She turned back to him, still seeming dreamy.

'Your . . .' He pointed, half standing, half crouching, and then he looked away again, thinking: *I can't believe I just did that.* It wasn't as though it was anyone's business – not as though her underwear was showing, or there was anyone here but the flies to notice.

'Oh?' He heard her wonder; and then he heard that laugh of hers: 'My heavens, can't even dress myself.' She laughed and laughed, as he made an effort not to watch her fixing those buttons, returning to the crouch and the tomatoes as though he might watch them at their growing. 'You must think I'm mad,' she said.

He did, sort of, but he said: 'No. Easy enough thing to do.'

'Yes.' Her tone grew as quickly serious: 'Especially easy when you're distracted.'

She crouched beside him once more and looked into the twisted heap of vines and wire beyond the tomatoes: 'It's going to be quite a job getting that in order, isn't it?'

'Not too big a job,' Jack replied. 'It's mostly blackberry, and not much at that. Could be worse. Takes over whole farms, this stuff, but you've got to it early. Chop it back, get some caustic soda painted on it, and it'll die off.'

'Poison it?' Grace Lovelee sounded alarmed.

'Yeah,' said Jack, and thought to calm her worry: 'It's not a dangerous poison.'

'Dangerous to the plant, though,' she said, frowning at it.

'Yeah,' said Jack, curious. 'No more dangerous to the plant than pulling it out of the ground. Same result. But a lot easier if you poison it. They're bast—' He just managed to stop himself from describing the blackberry as the bastard king of weeds it was. 'They're hard to shift once they settle in.' *Worse than whitefellers.*

'Oh.' She kept frowning at the vines, little white flowers strung along them, bees dancing all around collecting their gold-dust pollen. She said: 'Art won't like the idea of poison.'

'Fair enough,' Jack replied, wondering what sort of farmer doesn't need a bit of poison from time to time; he wondered at the man he'd seen smashing together that structure near the river, by the old schoolhouse: four-by-four posts all standing to attention in two lots of two lines like a slipway for Noah's next ark. Wanting to get to know these weird neighbours, he asked her: 'What's your husband been building then, ay?'

She turned that dazzling smile on him as she said: 'That's his nursery, or at least it's going to be, for the young fruit trees, and seed-raising. He'll put a canvas shade across the top, protecting them from the high sun. He's got it all worked out.' Then her sweet face darkened again: 'I hope it all works out for him.'

Jack wasn't sure why he said what he said next, but for a trace of worry for this woman slipping through his mind; worry like she was a lamb straggling from the mob: 'You need a hand, you know where to find me.'

'That's very kind,' she said. 'I'll tell Art. He'll be pleased to know he needn't advertise with the labour agent, hm?' She threw him a glance, some kind of twinkle in it, as though she was the one who had it all worked out, and Jack nearly fell off his heels: these people might really give him some work? But before he could clarify that, she asked him another question, pointing under one of the thick rambling arches of the blackberry bush: 'That's more of that burr grass there as well, isn't it?'

'Yeah, that's right.' Jack nodded at the spindly clump of the stuff. 'You want to dig them ones out or they'll spread, too.'

She knelt as she set her little spade on it and said, plain and straight as she dug: 'Art is sometimes not well. I don't usually mention anything about it to people, but you're not just people, are you. Since you were a soldier, I'm sure you know what I mean – probably more than even I do. He's all go, or all stop. Today, he's all stop.'

Jack nodded again, and with some genuine sympathy, though he didn't really know what she meant.

'Nothing wrong with stopping now and again,' she went on, digging round the base of another clump: 'If we all learned to stop for one – stop for the one who is stopped – then we'd all be better off, wouldn't we, hm?' She told the earth: 'And there wouldn't have been a damn war in the first place.'

My oath. My bloody oath. Jack was stuck there on his heels, struck by the uncommon wisdom of this woman, when she looked over her shoulder at him and said: 'The more of these burr things I dig up, the more I seem to see – and now I need something to gather them all in. Could you, please —'

She sat back on her own heels then, knees in the

dust, her pretty dress getting all dirty; she blinked at him: 'I was going to ask you to get my basket from the kitchen, but I left it with Mr McGlynn, across the way. You wouldn't mind fetching it for me, would you?'

Jack couldn't think of anything he'd rather do less than see that gun-slinging shit McGlynn.

'I mean, if it's not too much trouble.' Grace Lovelee blinked at him again. 'I don't fancy traipsing back . . .'

He looked at her kneeling there in the dirt; such a nice lady. Probably nothing would be too much trouble for a woman like her, he supposed.

'Oh – God.' She slapped the side of her leg. 'Please, ignore that. Listen to me, talking to you as though you're my servant – that's *not* what I meant. Or perhaps it was – I just forget where I am sometimes. It's different in England – women ask men to do things all the time and they do them. Well, for women like me, anyway. Or they did, once upon a time. What I really meant was that it's hot now, and I'm too hot to be bothered. And I probably shouldn't be digging in the garden. I should go and make lunch for Art – make him eat something, at least. You must think I'm awful for asking such a thing of you.'

Jesus, no. Jack could barely shake his head he was so taken by the woman, and he told her, despite himself: 'I don't mind. I'll go and get your basket, don't worry.'

'Are you sure you don't mind?' Grace Lovelee asked him with her beautiful, weary-wise eyes.

He knew somewhere in all this he was being strung and played but he was too intrigued to say anything else except: 'No. It's all right. I don't mind.'

Maybe she wanted to avoid McGlynn herself; *that* he could understand.

He set off, up the track through the vineyard, but it wasn't until he was nearly at McGlynn's gate that he realised there'd been a tin bucket near the back step he could have got for her to put all the burr grass in. Come to think of it, there'd been a wicker washing basket there too, by the clothesline post, only a spit from where they'd been bending over the weeds.

Not to worry; he was here now. Wary nevertheless, once inside the gate, he skirted his way round the homestead yard, hoping to catch sight of McGlynn before the bloke caught sight of him. He followed the path of the long-lost track that once led to the old general store; made a detour down to the large, lone emu bush here that was in full flower – a cloud of flowers, it was. No point not taking advantage, he supposed. He plucked one of the little pink, trumpet-shaped blooms, careful not to break the bulb of nectar that sat at its base; this particular bush always seemed to have the most delicious juice, and he wondered if that was because it held this patch of dark red ground on its own, sharing it only with one of the stone stumps left behind by the store.

He raised the bulb to his lips; the insides of his cheeks tingled and watered with anticipation.

Then he saw McGlynn: a way off, sitting on an upturned crate by this near end of one of his orchard rows, with that damn rifle of his between his knees.

Sitting there taking pot shots at the birds, are you? So Jack thought.

But he was wrong: and it was his turn to blink now, not quite believing what he thought he might be seeing.

McGlynn had the muzzle of that gun held to his mouth – held within his teeth.

'No!' Jack shouted.

His own tongue sang with the taste of iron, his mind filled with thundering hooves, the screaming of beasts, all beasts, as he began to run.

SNOW

His vision faded around a blue-grey smudge that sat upon the west horizon. There was not much otherwise going on in his mind: it was more a sensation that had overwhelmed him, the feeling that's got after many days without sleep, though he'd slept like a bag of bricks these past several nights. It was a feeling like acid in the veins; all brittle and riven edges, all flaking and crumbling away.

He wasn't even thinking of Moz.

He just wanted this feeling to stop; this feeling that nothing good could ever come from his hand or his heart; that these oranges and lemons could not rescue him: they were only a fragile monument to his vanity that he might do anything of any use at all.

He wanted to drift out along the river – any river – and away into the centre of that blue-grey smudge.

The rough steel wings of the foresight scraped the top of his mouth; he could smell the linseed oil in the timber of the barrel casing; his thumb rested on the trigger. At the next breath he'd lean into it; at the next breath he'd do it and be gone.

'What the fucken hell are you doing?'

At first he thought it was Stu, but it couldn't have been – and Stu never sounded that angry.

'Get that fucken thing out of your mouth – you fucken idiot.'

Snow looked up to his left, to find the source of the voice: it was that blackfeller – that blackfeller always mooching around.

Things happened quickly from there: Snow McGlynn suddenly became aware of what he had indeed been doing – and he was as suddenly embarrassed to have been caught in such a shameful position. He turned the gun on the one who sought to stop him: this frowning brown face looking down at him.

'Get fucked.' Snow made a firmer point of that gun as he stood, but his words fell like lead on the ground between them.

The black man didn't move but for a flaring of his nostrils; he squared at Snow and said: 'Well, go on, then. I've got nothing to lose.'

Something in that challenge infuriated Snow: that this barefoot, scrap-of-nothing black thought he was bastard enough to shoot him in cold blood. And with the too-hot flight of logic that accompanies all dire distress, Snow chucked the gun away and threw a punch instead.

The black man dodged the fist and pushed his own into Snow's chest. 'Yeah, I'll have you,' he said: 'Come on – go again.'

There was little fight left in him now, and Snow stumbled backwards, but the black man kept at him, shouting: 'Have a go, you pink-arsed cunt – have a go!' And he pushed him once more so he fell to the ground.

Snow raised a hand, half in surrender, half in anticipation of a blow, and he shouted back: 'Stop! I've got no argument with you.'

The black man stood over him, black shadow against the near-white, high-sun sky: 'Oh yes, you fucken do.'

'What?' Snow was getting fearful now. 'I haven't done anything to you.'

'That what you reckon?' The man spat into the dust by his shoulder. 'You've taken my land, my home, my family. But yeah – you've not done nothing to me, have you.'

Snow didn't know what to make of that, other than supposing this bloke was right off his head, and maybe in a state far more murderous than the one he himself had been in just now.

But the black man only said: 'I've come for Mrs Lovelee's basket – she wants it returned. Where is it?'

'On the verandah,' Snow said, too stunned to chat about it further, 'out the back.'

He watched the black man walk up to the house, an unhurried but efficient pace; he watched him disappear behind the thicket of old rosebushes there, and come out the other side, with that basket. He watched him go up the track and out the gate.

He might have wondered if he'd imagined all that but his elbow stung from having fallen on it. He got to his feet, in a daze. He picked up his gun: beyond time he put this filthy piece of shit away.

As he neared the house to do just that, his mind still numb from shock, he saw his horse, yarded in her pen there to the south, where she had shade and water, but no food – he'd been about to blow his own head off, but he'd not thought to put out any hay for the horse. How could he have done that? How could he have been so selfish? The horse had a name when he bought her in town but he'd forgotten it; he only ever called her Girl. Who was he?

He kept on going around to the back of the house, where he saw something somehow worse, and somehow an answer, too: the white bundle, left here on the verandah boards – it was the bread that Grace Lovelee had brought him, but wrapped as it was in her linen cloth, it looked like a little baby.

His knees just about gave way at the sight of it, and he sat down on the step there by the loaf.

He shook with the relief that floods the body on its surprise at being alive.

Then, at last, and for the very first time, Snow McGlynn began to cry.

GRACE

'Kettles and pans, say the bells of Saint Ann's. Three beans and one pea, say the bells of Saint Steve's. Oh me, oh my . . .' Grace laughed as the song rambled away from her. 'I'm just making it up now.'

She was standing at the kitchen sink, filling the kettle, trying not to miss the electric one they'd had in Sydney. There was no electricity here in Sunshine, of course, not even a lightbulb; no street lighting in Bourke, either. In a way, it wasn't so different from the villages that lay outside Chippenham – Slaughterford, Thickwood, The Shoe, you'd not have a lightbulb between that lot – but the distances here in Australia . . . Ah, the distances . . . Whether in Wiltshire's quaint limestone cottages, or the fashionable apartments of London squares, people sat close, and closer still towards Christmas, against the drear, against the cold. They didn't necessarily converse – God forbid – but they were there: visible.

Here, framed within the kitchen window, a line of dark rainclouds rose above the rust-dusted land like a blue brushstroke, a mountain range made tiny by forever. The thought that there might be fewer than a dozen souls between herself and that faraway rain – that there might be none but Jack Bell and Joseph McGlynn – was both exciting and shocking.

'Electrifying,' she whispered through her smile, and almost called out to Art, before telling herself, again: *No. Leave him.* He remained in such a sound sleep, and there was no more sound medicine. *Such a temptation, though, isn't it?* she mused: *To wake the soundly sleeping one, just to tell them how beautifully sound they are.*

Her smile curled then around the shape of Jack Bell, walking towards the house as though he might have been pulling those clouds along with him. Now, there was a beautiful man in all his shapes and sinews – and a haunted one. She wondered what horrors had caused him to choose a lonely riverbank for his home; she'd find out, too, eventually, she hoped. In the meantime, she stoked the stove and placed the kettle on it, trying not to miss the convenience of piped gas, too. Even the making of a cup of tea was slow out here – and perhaps just as it should be. Just as they all needed it to be.

Leaving the kettle to boil, she stepped out onto the verandah, and waved to Jack as he neared: 'Would you like a cup of tea?'

The man gave a low wave in return, holding up the basket with his other hand – her basket, which she'd quite forgotten about now. He placed it on the ground by the back step and said: 'No thanks, Mrs – ah, Grace. I'll be off.'

And off he went, straight-backed and in some way slouching, downcast, at the same time.

Hm. Grace wondered what his change in mood might have meant, if that McGlynn fellow had been rude or mean – such an odd, gruff man, he was – but she thought better of asking anything about it right at that moment. She watched Jack Bell walk on instead, dragging that long cloud behind him – or perhaps dragging it up the sky, she thought as she looked back at forever, at the blue cloud mountain rising over that wide western plain.

A storm? she wondered at it, and indeed that's what it was; she stood there for a little while, watching it gather. But as she squinted she saw something else out there against the sun-bright blackening clouds – something gold and moving slowly.

Moving closer. It looked like three golden leaves, glimmering, and somehow being drawn across the furthest reaches of their rear paddock. What *was* it?

'Where's my cup of tea, woman!' The deep voice of a man crashed along the verandah, and though she knew it was Art, she jumped and spun and barked a laugh: 'Oh you!'

He grinned, sleepily, his dark hair all over the place on his head; he yawned and stretched out his long, strong arms.

She said: 'Aren't you wonderful.'

'I am.' He gave himself a scratch behind the ear.

'Darling.' She pointed out at the golden leaves: 'What's that, can you see? What's that moving out there?'

From behind her, he roped his arms around her waist and rested his chin on the top of her head: 'Where?'

'There – see?'

'Ha!' he said when he saw it, squinting too. 'Land ho! I do believe they are ships of the desert, my love. Camels.'

'Camels!' She was delighted. She'd heard several times already that the district was being overrun with the creatures, set loose by Afghan hawkers driven out of business by trains and motor-trucks, and now those camels had gone feral, making pests of themselves breaking fences and trampling crops, but seeing them here, in this dramatically fantastical storm-light, well, it was like a circus coming into town – albeit a very small one. How strange, how incongruous, and yet how fitting they seemed. 'How magical.' She sighed, leaning back against Art's chest, imagining the caravans said to have traversed these vast expanses, carrying everything from finest silks to scrubbing brushes across seas of red sand the size of Britain and more. 'The three wise camels,' she mused, squeezing the edges of her husband's broad, tanned hands, pressing them to her belly full of Christmas wishes: *Please*.

'Did I hear you talking to someone just now?' Art asked her, and she turned in his arms.

'Yes,' she told him. 'A neighbour, but not McGlynn. A man called Jack Bell – native fellow, I presume, though I don't exactly know. He lives on the riverbank.' She glanced back over at the storm, concerned now that he would be out in this weather. 'We really should invite him to stay, but I'm not sure he'd accept the invitation.'

Art laughed; how she loved that sound, and this laugh in particular: a steady, rumbling chuckle that burrowed and quivered through every depth of her own being. That sleep truly had done him a world of good; she beamed into his gentled drowse as he replied: 'I can't imagine why anyone would be reluctant to stay with us.'

'Seriously, darling,' she said. 'I'm a little worried about him – and a lot intrigued. He seems a decent chap – helped me this morning in the garden, advising me on the weeds. But he . . . Hm.' She wasn't sure and yet she was: 'I think he's one of us.'

'One of us?' That brought Art a little more into the here and now of his waking-up. 'That might be unlikely,' he said. 'There weren't any natives in the army – not ours. No black Anzacs. *Defence Act* wouldn't take darkies of any kind.'

Darkies – what a patronising, belittling snick of a word she thought that was; but she let it go and told her husband: 'He was wearing old khakis – the bottom half, at least.'

Art shrugged: 'Probably from a government store. There's an Aboriginal reserve or what have you over at Brewarrina – he's probably come from there.'

'Hm,' she said in some vague agreeance, but she really didn't think so. The man had murmured it so quietly she couldn't quite hear, but she was sure he'd said he'd served with the Light Horse.

'It's a hard time for the blacks.' Art gazed out towards the river. 'Not that I know much about it, but it does seem that angry white men who've been betrayed by their country need to believe they're not the lowest of the low – they need to be made to feel that way so they don't start shooting at each other and tearing up the whole show. It's always been bad for blacks, but I'd say it's worse now.'

She knew too little of these Aboriginal people to guess at how, but wondered if men were shooting each other in the backstreets of Birmingham and Berlin – probably. Betrayal bears the cruellest fruit. The brawls she'd seen behind the lines – over a woman, a beer, half a cigarette – one doesn't simply turn that off on the ship home. There's not much worse than men who should be friends fighting each other because – why? Because they were all torn apart inside, and those Aussies, always and ever so boastful for their unbreakable mateship, were not immune – indeed, she recalled they seemed to have served and received the worst of such black eyes. She wondered for the millionth time how on earth it was that Art, in his always and ever gentleness, had survived at all. Must have been the sunshine he carried around, somewhere in there, thread-thin too regularly, but there – and here, right here, in his happy-sad smile.

A shiver ran up the back of her neck, as it did whenever the thought occurred: how had *she* survived? That sensation of life leaving under her hands, her useless, helpless hands, would never leave her: men, so young and beautiful, all of them. How did it not drive her insane? Perhaps women found it easier to cope because they were never asked to kill or maim. She was never called upon to harm another – not that she was so full of the milk of human kindness that she'd never done so. She'd bullied a girl once at school, for no reason other than to try it, and she could be quite impatient, quite cutting when faced with another's wilful stupidity. But she'd never been paid wages to cause another pain – not counting all the pain she'd inflicted in the attempt to close wounds, not counting that one young man she'd slapped so hard in the attempt to bring him back from his hysterical delirium she could still feel the sting of it inside the bones of her hand.

But she had survived, so had Art, and she held his happy-sad smile within her stinging hand right now: 'You're all right, aren't you.'

'I am.' He nodded, with a twitch of an eyebrow: wry. 'Some strange woman came in and took mad, passionate advantage of me this morning.'

'Lucky you!' She kissed his cheeks and the tip of his nose; his slightly crooked nose broken long ago not in war but in collision with a cricket bat, wicketkeeping, for his old club at Stanmore, the names of half his team having more recently shifted their gold block lettering from premiership victors of the living to the honour roll of the dead hanging on the walls of Petersham town hall.

'Care to dance?' His arms were already whisking her along the verandah boards.

'Not until you've eaten something.' She whisked him towards the kitchen door. 'Something substantial.'

'Always looking after me, aren't you.' He held her closer in gratitude.

'Someone must.' Sometimes, too oftentimes, she really did think the wounds of the world might fall apart again without her holding them closer still. At least, she knew Art would.

*

But Art was all right, he truly was, so it seemed. They'd enjoyed a fortnight of ordinary Artness, October folding into November, the longest he'd gone without a mood for as long as she could re-member, and she knew better than to think anything more of it than what it was: wonderful.

And so had been the rain: each afternoon those clouds would sweep up over the plain, drenching the soil and singing on the tin roof of the house for a good ten or fifteen minutes before rolling cheerfully onward. The earth deepened all its colours, all its own pleasure, the reds of the earth redder, the greens of the scrabbly grass greener and spreading across the land like hands seeking hands, and in every puddle stood flowers of a kind she'd never seen before: white globes atop tall, slender stems, their petals unfurling like feathery suns.

Oh boy but it was getting hot, though, the nights sticky and the days reaching such a searing temperature she couldn't imagine what it might be like in summer here; and yet she could, and she welcomed the prospect, the very *foreignness* of such heat, when in her mind's eye she could see her mother at home wrapping a favourite cashmere scarf around her neck and face until only her eyes peeped over it. Grace had written to her only the day before with the certain declaration she would not be cooking a roast turkey for Christmas dinner this year, not here in Sunshine. She didn't know what they might have instead, though. Tomato sandwiches? Why not? And, possibly, seventeen gin-and-tonics.

When she and Art had arrived in Sydney almost a year ago, the summer had been unusually cool, and so had the yuletide table of Art's parents; as an only child herself, Grace had been accustomed to small festivities, but never with such a lack of actual festivity. She could understand the pall of grief that lay across every surface, of course; she knew that here was a son and a young country brutally blooded, irrevocably changed, sixty thousand lost to a war a million miles away, but she had felt like pointing out that the United Kingdom had lost ten times more and had not exactly forced Australia to join them at gunpoint. She'd kept her mouth shut, though, like the good little Pommy girl she was. 'They don't like me,' Grace had whispered in the night. 'They don't like anyone,' Art had sighed, a well-versed regret. Her in-laws were, for better or worse, sour people – people that hadn't, when all was said and done, lost much more in all the boundless tragedy than a few clients of their petty, suburban accountancy firm who'd had the temerity to get themselves killed overseas. Life was too brutally short to think too much more about them. Art didn't, and he didn't want a repeat of that Christmas dinner, either. She could certainly promise him that. This Christmas, she decided, would be a ritual reinvented by Grace

Lovelee alone. A true celebration of new life.

With these first inklings, she decided this morning to begin sandpapering the front flyscreen door, stripping it back in preparation for its new coat of paint. She'd already chosen the colour, to match the original – Art had brought home the paint selection chart from the hardware store in Bourke. 'Pale Blue', it was called, this colour, according to the Aladdin paint company at least, and the name did its prettiness no justice, she thought once more as she looked over at the tin waiting there on the kitchen table. Over this past fortnight, the house had revealed more and more of its original prettiness: tiles surrounding the hearth in the rear parlour showed themselves after a scrub to have been glazed with an exquisitely detailed pattern of grapes and vine leaves; an excursion under the back verandah turned up a handsome marble bench seat and a three-foot-tall sculpture of a cherub posing on a scroll-topped plinth. While cleaning out the fitted cupboard in the laundry, two creased and faded photographs had slid out from under a pile of old drapes, all stinking with rat doings: one showed a horse by a fence; the other, this house, with a title marked beneath it in white block lettering – 'Kiriella' – because even its name must be pretty. And then, while attacking the garden-jungle again, she'd found an ornately crafted bronze-wire birdcage in the midst of the blackberry tangle; of course they'd never put a bird in such a thing, so instead it now stood in welcome on the front verandah with Art's moth-eaten boyhood toy monkey leaning jauntily by the open door. She had no idea now, though, where she'd put her sheets of sandpaper – for the flyscreen door.

Hadn't Art brought them in with the paint? Perhaps he had but had then pinched them for himself, she thought – *I'll go and pinch them back.*

She donned her floppy hat against the scorching, almost midday sun. 'Darling!' she called across the yard as she walked towards the river and the potting shed he'd knocked together beside his now completed colonnades of shade. This potting shed was a place where many things seemed to have disappeared to since its construction seven days ago: three teacups; two spoons and a fork; her nail scissors and all of her silk stockings, including a new pair purchased on leaving Sydney, which she hadn't yet worn. 'Darling Art, do you have my sandpaper?' she called, not sure where he was, as she couldn't see him anywhere.

But she could see his colonnades – and oh how she might forgive him anything at the sight.

Beneath their canvas sails his seed beds lay, and along the centre of this nearest colonnade, raised above his trays of strawberry, rockmelons and honeydew just gone in, a trough made of tin ran full length, and hanging over its edges either side were strips of those silk stockings of hers, carrying water drip by drip – at optimum quantity, so Art said. The whole thing looked like a gigantic centipede, and God did it thrill her from her toes to her fingertips. 'The Arthur Adam Lovelee Drip Irrigation System brought to you by Kayser Rolette Hosiery,' he'd said. 'Bona fide genius,' she'd said. He might have been mad, this husband of hers, but oh he was clever.

If anything was going to help heal the insult and injury of his talents at engineering having been used to plot Death's trenches and mine tunnels, surely this was it.

But, in fact, this was only one half of it. He had yet to build his sprinklers for the citrus and stone-fruit and sultana rootstock yet to arrive. The labour agent in town had been having difficulty finding a truck to bring the young trees from the train, after their trip up from Nyngan, one hundred and thirty miles, and then quickly from the station so as to avoid boiling the delicate cargo prior to arrival – but Art was in no rush now. Grace smiled at the first of the germinating honeydew, tiny lime squiggles coming up for light, for life, for air, as she called her husband again: 'Art! Where art Art! My hearty Art!'

Still no answer, but that didn't worry her: like many men who'd spent any time on the Western Front, he was a little bit deaf.

She popped her head into the potting shed but he wasn't there either; her sandpaper was, though, and she pocketed that on her way through, continuing down to the river, to see if he was there.

Now, Grace's hearing, like all her senses, was exceptionally acute, and she heard what she thought was music coming from the old schoolhouse a little way away – and not music she'd heard out here before.

A harmonica . . .

Had he bought himself a new musical toy? It wouldn't have surprised her. But as she took a step closer, she heard her dear Art singing now above the mellowly lilting tune. My, my was his a honeyed voice, so rich, so deep – it was golden syrup on toasted crumpets. He was singing a song she'd certainly heard before, because it was one of those composed by none other than himself, and she knew every word:

'I met a marvellous English girl
And she was sparkling fair.
Red roses kissed her smiling cheek
And silken was her hair.
The sun lit every path she took
And danced in every curl.
Her eyes were bright with love and light,
Oh that lovely English girl.'

'My own light gone, my heart worn through,
She came and sat by me.
She took my hand inside her own,
She set my spirit free.
She brought the sun inside her smile,
She danced, though I could not.
She coaxed me from my misery
And returned what I'd forgot.

'A miracle, she was, my English girl.
She raised me from the dead.
She found me in pieces, smashed to bits,
And put me together again.
Her small hand upon my khaki sleeve,
Her courage large, my pearl.
She fixes all my brokenness,
My marvellous English girl.'

There wasn't much these days that could bring Grace a tear, but that song did it every time, and not just because the sentiment was the prettiest thing of all. It cut through her usual steady resolve, as it reminded her in some fundamental way that she'd have preferred not to always have to be so bloody marvellous.

'By gee . . .' another voice offered hushed appreciation, a man's voice, and one she recognised to be Jack Bell's by its unrushed, tender rasp, as he added: 'There's a song for the ages, ay.'

Indeed. She couldn't see either of them from where she was, by the side wall of the schoolhouse, except for the toe of one of Art's scuffed-up work boots. His legs stretched out, he must have been sitting with his back to the front wall, Jack Bell somewhere with him there. She hadn't seen Jack since the day he'd helped her in the garden, though she'd wondered where he might be; she'd searched for him along the riverbank but found no sign of him except a bundle of charcoaled logs where his campfire had been. She'd wondered if he'd moved on; she'd wondered if that so-and-so McGlynn had caused him to. But perhaps he'd only been staying in the old schoolhouse all along, to keep out of the squally rainstorms. This thought caused a whisper of happiness to slip through her, like sunlight on her soul, like the warm breeze at her back. She wasn't sure why, except that it seemed somehow right: that he was here, and here with Art.

She heard Jack Bell murmur something about not meeting any sweethearts in Palestine, 'My nurse had a big hairy moustache . . .' And Art laughed. They laughed together for a good minute solid, like boys. Whatever this exchange was between them, it was an intimate one.

Grace left them to it, making her way back to the house, watching the rise of the clouds as she walked. She winked at Monkey in his cage on the verandah, impersonating Art: 'What do you reckon, then, hm?' Then she set to work on the flyscreen door.

She wasn't sure how long she'd been at it, but she'd unscrewed the door from its frame and was almost finished sanding the whole front side when Art called up from the yard, impersonating himself in caricature: 'Put the kettle on then, missus.'

'What a good idea, darling.' She grinned at him as he neared: 'Two sugars, please.'

He would happily oblige, but he sat on the step by her first, his hat on his knee. 'I met that native fellow Jack Bell,' he said.

'Did you?' she replied, as if she didn't know; and she kept on with the sandpaper, around one of the fretworked swirls.

'Yes,' Art told her. 'I saw him harvesting some leaves off a shrub, some sort of bush tea, in that patch of scrub where the track towards Brewarrina winds east beyond our fence. I was curious, we got chatting, and, well, he's an interesting chap. You know, he served with the Light Horse.'

'You don't say.'

'I do.' He told her: 'He did his most spectacular bit in the charge on Beersheba.' Art paused and added: 'Rough stuff there, it was.'

'Hm.' Grace stopped her sandpapering and sat back on her heels. She never went to the Near East herself, but she knew enough second-hand to nod at her husband's gravity with some understanding: the capture of Beersheba had been a bloodbath as horrific as any of them. *All those horses. . .* Such wholesale slaughter of such innocence. Grace had seen too much of all that in France, carcasses left wherever they fell, eternally unpeaceful, still steaming under circling crows. *What on earth for?*

'Hm.' Art gazed back out towards his colonnades. 'Only got worse for our Jack Bell. When he returned home, to Queensland initially, he found the police had taken his child away.'

'What?' Grace wasn't sure she'd heard that correctly. 'Taken his what away?'

'His child, yes,' Art replied, and then explained: 'The child was bundled off to who knows where. A common thing these days, for Aborigines, half-castes generally, and especially if a child isn't being cared for.'

'Was the child not being cared for?' she asked, still not quite fathoming.

'Well, I don't know about that, do I.' Art shrugged, and then he sighed: 'But Jack Bell said his wife was devoted to her – their daughter. Smashed his little family to bits. How about that, hm?'

'How about that, all right.' Grace was almost disbelieving that any such thing could happen to anyone. 'But what can he do, to put it right?'

'Nothing,' said Art, and in such a matter-of-fact way dread rippled through her. 'Aborigines are controlled by the state,' her husband explained further and more dreadfully. 'They don't get a say in these sorts of things. Or anything, really. They're told where to live, where to go, what to do. The little girl is probably in an orphans' home now, or something like that.'

'Oh. Is that so.' Grace didn't know what to do

with this information. As an Englishwoman, and an intelligent, too-worldly one, she was not naïve to the consequences of being on the losing side of Empire, but she'd never heard of anything so deplorable before. What was Jack Bell? A horse? The man had served this Empire and was now both homeless and family-less. There had to be something she could do, to put it right; but she didn't know what that might be – yet.

'Anyway,' said Art, getting to his feet again, 'for a few bob, Jack has agreed to help me prepare the field for planting out the melons.'

'Oh good.' There's one thing they could do for him: pay him. Pay him agency-rate wages, without the agency-rate fee deductions. Yes, Grace Lovelee might have been relatively fresh off the boat as regards the Australian way – of arcane labour laws and state incarceration of blameless children – but she could break a rule as well as any of them.

'He's keen to help me with the sprinkler rig-up, too,' Art added as he stepped around her and into the house. 'Keen on things mechanical. Good bloke, decent sort of fellow . . .' His voice trailed away as he left her.

She smiled to herself: God – ever almightily capricious in His bestowal of gifts – certainly moved mysteriously here. Her darling Art, it appeared, had made a friend. In all the time she'd known him, he'd not really had one of them – not a friend that wasn't hers, not a friend who was alive, or who had survived the gulf that gaped between those who'd served and those who'd stayed behind.

A friend. Perhaps. But even the perhaps was wonderful enough.

The warm thought of it uncoiled a tendril of some secret joy from her very centre.

She returned to her sandpapering; Art brought her out that cup of tea and then fell into a doze before drinking his own – she could hear him snoring from the lounge. As the afternoon stretched, there came a slow rolling rumble of thunder, and another, and rain pattered and plinked on the tin awning above her, teeming a moment before it swept on; the welcome swallows zoomed about up in the rafters, protecting their precious eggs: three of them, there were. She'd got up on a step ladder a few days ago to see: three perfect little eggs, of palest pink and speckled grey.

Yes, horror was everywhere, injustice was everywhere, the whole globe over, but, thought Grace, new life is *here*. New life in this most ancient of lands.

She was almost finished sanding the back of the flyscreen door when a man on a horse appeared at the gate, dismounting to let himself in. A policeman: instantly recognisable by the smart white britches and navy tunic. It wasn't the same fellow who'd come out to visit them when they'd first arrived, though – the rather dopey but congenial, hunch-shouldered Sergeant Greavy. This policeman was sharper in bearing, young and leaner all over, and he narrowed his eyes as he touched the brim of his helmet in greeting: 'Afternoon, Mrs Lovelee, is it?'

'Good afternoon.' She stood. She couldn't have said why precisely, but it was distrust at first sight.

'Sergeant Brandell,' he said. *Saaargeant Braaandell* had an outback drawl that sounded like it had been put through a circular saw, and he placed the heel of his tall black boot on the bottom step, in a none-too-subtle display of authority. 'From Bourke,' he added with an air of arrogance, and unnecessarily, as it was unlikely that he'd have come from anywhere else.

'And what brings you out this way?' she asked, daring to send a little arrogance back at him.

'I'm looking for a black called Bell, Jack Bell, said to be living out here on the river. He's wanted by the police.'

'Wanted?' Grace didn't know what to think of that. She'd stared down far worse than this fancied-up bobby, but he sent a bolt of fear through her, oh yes, he did.

He said: 'That's right. Wanted. By order of the District Superintendent. I have a warrant for Bell's arrest from Bourke Police Court.'

'A warrant for whom?' She feigned confusion, but didn't have to feign too hard. If Jack Bell had done something wrong, it could be nothing next to the wrongs that had been done to him – surely?

'A man called Jack Bell,' the policeman repeated. 'Six feet tall, about thirty years of age. Aborigine. Unlawful vagrant. Possibly dangerous.'

'Dangerous?' She could make no sense of that at all; the man she'd met had had too much of a gentleness about him. *Surely?*

'Yes, dangerous,' the policeman repeated himself once more. 'Any blacks at large and unsupervised on any areas of settlement are considered dangerous.'

'Dangerous.' She sent the word back at this young man who quite possibly did not share her own understandings of danger. She told him: 'I'm sure I haven't seen the man you describe.'

'Seen who?' Art appeared beside her now, shambling inside a yawn and saluting down at the policeman: 'Hello there, you must be Brandell, are you? The new chap?' He was pouring on the charm: 'Come in! Come in! I was just about to crack open a bottle or two – join me, won't you?'

'Don't mind if I do,' the young policeman swaggered up the stairs, full of his own importance, and as he clomped his way into the house, Art gave her a wink and some pretence of his own: 'Go and fetch my cigarettes, will you, love – I left them in the shed.'

He did not need to issue any further directive: she had to go and warn Jack.

Her steps were quick across the yard; the very image of the dutiful wife.

But when she got down to the old schoolhouse, there was no one there. Even the remains of the campfire had vanished. All trace of Jack Bell was gone.

BLOOM

BLOOM

JACK

There comes a time when several hundred corellas can do a man a favour, and this was one of those times. After the passing of the rain, they rose as one from the trees on the northern corner of the river, drying off their wings in the last furnace blast of late-afternoon sun. The flock made a wide arc south towards the Lovelees' place, all screaming and squawking as they flew, putting on such a show that not even a copper with murder on his mind could have fought the urge to look up at them.

Jack had grabbed the little he possessed: his old army great coat; frying pan; billy can; tin mug; the cannister full of lemon-bush tea he'd only just harvested from the whitewoods down by the Brewarrina track. He dragged a scrappy old branch over the fire he'd not got the chance to light – *thank Christ* – and made his way along the scungy, well-littered stretches of the riverbank, trying to keep his footprints hidden, keeping as low as he could, out of all view.

That copper, he must have brought that horse of his creeping through the storm, right down to the schoolhouse, nosing about, wanting to catch Jack unawares – and so he did, until that horse let out a snort to tell him what was up. Jack had barely had time to scramble through the hole in the floor. He'd been warned by Greavy that this new bloke would come for him, and here he was, shiny buttons and all.

I am not getting roped in, Jack promised himself, crawling out from between the foundation stumps as he heard the copper move off towards the Lovelees'. *I will not be chained up on that station like a criminal. I'm not a flaming criminal – not in any way other than what the army demanded of me.*

No more than Art Lovelee was; Jack had seen all that plain enough in the man's eyes, not to mention his throwaway line of having earned a place as a basket case in Flanders: it's the murdering that turns your mind inside out and has your soul absconding AWL in fright. They'd recognised each other at first sight. No words for that.

And none for this, either: Jack Bell skulking off,

running from the law, a felon for living on his own land – for being fool enough to believe things could be any other way.

He ducked under the rickety timbers of the wool wharf, his feet sinking into the cool mud, catching his breath; catching his hopelessness.

It was time, yes it was time, to hand himself in.

Hang himself, one way or another. Be done with it.

He closed his eyes against the slash of sun on the water, silver, white hot, his blood pumping molten rock. A frog croaked somewhere behind him where the wharf met the bank, where moss grew in shadows dank and permanent; the corellas returned, chattering, rustling all the branches above, as Jack Bell contemplated giving up.

How do you know when enough is enough? How do you know when you've stepped over that line between righteousness and delusion? How do you know if you're right or wrong in the first place? Maybe he had no business digging in here, he began to think in his distress. Maybe he was just another truculent, non-compliant black undeserving of anything more than what he had: nothing.

But it wasn't true, and he knew it. He was a good man; he'd been a good soldier, he'd always been a good worker, and he'd been a good husband, too. How had he been brought to this? He knew the answer to that one as well – he knew it was all about the land, who claimed it, who owned it, and the law always falling on the side of a white man, be it the bastard squatter who raped his grandmother or King George – but knowing it didn't change a thing. It was simple, really, and nothing personal, not to them; but it was everything personal to him. It was branded on him in his name, like it might have been on any jumbuck's arse or implement of farming: property of Isiah Bell, who'd come and gone, leaving a trail of destruction in his wake. Jack's heart smashed around the enormity of all his losses, and at the sorest centre of his most essential self lay his longing for his little daughter, Mary – the too-overwhelming thought that he'd likely never see her again.

And he wanted to die.

It's time, he told himself again.

He'd hand himself in quietly; if he was going to submit to defeat, then out at Brewarrina he'd at least be able to do it on good rations – he knew they got a meal of beef out there once a week. It had been a long time since he'd tasted damper, fresh and crusty from the coals; or butter and jam; or real tea.

He got out from under the wharf, tucked his shirt in, smoothed back his thick black hair with his hands. He was ready.

He stepped up the bank and, like a trap had been laid, there was that mad bastard McGlynn, waiting for him, looking ready, too – that damn rifle in his white-knuckled fist.

Jack's hands automatically leapt above his head, and he made no sound, except perhaps a sigh: *So, this is it.*

Then McGlynn said to him under a flint-eyed squint, 'Jesus, do you have to look at me like that?'

Like what? Jack had no idea what he was looking like or looking at.

'I'm not going to shoot you.' McGlynn pointed the muzzle away, up at the trees. 'I was just about to get into them birds.'

Idiot, Jack sighed again, but his hands were still raised above his head; he didn't know what to do.

'That you, Mr McGlynn?' And here came the copper too, up on his high horse, looming over them. 'This bloke giving you trouble?'

Both Jack and McGlynn frowned at him askance, but it was McGlynn who spoke: 'No trouble here.'

'Good,' said the copper, getting down from the saddle. 'Let's see that it stays that way.' He stared at

Jack, too young and too full of himself; Jack supposed he was the type with something to prove. He gave Jack a long, careful going-over with that stare and said: 'Are you the Abo called Bell?'

Jack looked away, repulsed by this young feller's tone. What can you do with that kind of disrespect? Where can you put it, to keep it at a distance?

'There's no trouble here,' McGlynn said again, and fiercer about it.

'Good.' The copper gave him a nod – that full of himself it was a wonder he didn't choke, as he told McGlynn, 'And there'll be even less trouble when this here Bell feller comes with me.'

'Goes with you? What for?' McGlynn didn't mind giving the police a bit of bastard, either.

'He's under arrest.' The young copper straightened and squared. 'I have a warr—'

'What's he done?' McGlynn fairly snarled it at him.

And the young copper paled then, though his voice remained steady: 'He's to be charged as an idle and disorderly person.'

'Get off,' said McGlynn with a flick of his wrist. 'This man is not idle – he works for me.'

There was some news for them all; Jack's eyes nearly fell out of his head.

'Oh?' the policeman said. 'I wasn't informed of that.'

'Well, you have been now, haven't you.' McGlynn gave him another get-off curl of the lip.

But the copper wasn't finished: 'Do you have a permit to employ him, from the Board?'

From the New South Wales Aborigines Protection Board, who, like their Queensland equivalent, did nothing in the way of protecting anyone from anything, unless it was to steal kids and wages and land in the name of the Commissioner of Police. Jack knew all about that, of course. When he'd first stepped foot off the ship in Brisbane, waiting on the station platform there for that train up to Rocky, he was greeted with a welcome-home newspaper telling him that the Australian Workers Union was now demanding that no Aborigine be employed anywhere by anyone ever at all – tricky, them blackfellers, undercutting white men's wages. Lest we forget. He'd thought it was a joke some-how, and nothing to do with him – he'd thought he'd have no trouble getting back into contract droving. *Ha!*

'No, I do not have a fucken permit.' McGlynn took a step closer to the copper, still clenching that rifle in his fist.

Shit. Jack didn't want any part of this.

The young bloke stood his ground: 'I suggest you consider making an application, at the court-house then, Mr McGlynn. It's a straightforward procedure. Failure to do so will incur an increased fine —'

'What do you mean "increased fine".'

'I mean greater than the fine you will receive for employing an Aborigine without a fucken permit in the first instance. You have twenty-eight days to make your application to the court. In the mean-time, you will be issued your fucken fine.'

Jack supposed McGlynn would have to buckle at that, take back the lie he'd just told, but he didn't.

He only nodded: 'Righto.' And told the copper, with some emphasis: 'See you later, then.'

Another brief staring competition ensued before the copper was back on that horse of his and head-ing off.

And Jack was asking McGlynn: 'What did you do that for?' He knew he wasn't owed any favours by this man; the last and only significant time they'd met, Jack had all but throttled him.

But McGlynn only shrugged and walked away, down along the wharf.

SNOW

'Thanks anyway,' the black man said at his back. This man called Bell. Snow didn't want to look at him: he was still embarrassed at having been sprung on the verge of blowing his own brains out, and remained unconvinced that his was a life worth saving. There was something else, too: the way this Aboriginal man looked at him: warily, like he was the enemy. Snow McGlynn might have been an angry and hate-filled bastard of the worst order, but he wasn't any man's enemy, and the contradiction in these two facts sent such a crashing discord through Snow's mind, he couldn't make head nor tail of it – a noise worse than these bastard birds, all thirty-seven million of them screaming and shrieking as the sun began to sink through the trees.

Snow turned at the end of the wharf and raised his gun.

'Don't do that,' this blackfeller Bell called out to him. 'Picking off one or two won't make any difference.'

Still, Snow picked out one, lining it up in the dead centre of his foresight, just wanting this bloke to piss off now.

But he didn't; and Snow couldn't fire, either: the bird moved and his vision blurred, searching out another.

'You got a stockwhip?' the bloke asked him, not going anywhere.

Snow couldn't look at him, but he asked: 'A what?' Not sure if he'd understood him.

'A stockwhip,' Bell said again. 'Get in under the trees and crack it for a good half hour or so. Same time every day, just as they're settling in. You've got to teach them – be regular about it. If you just take a couple of shots now and then, they don't know what you're on about. You've gotta really get in under them to get them to clear off – you've got to really give them the shits.'

Snow lowered the gun. Shooting at them had definitely achieved bugger all. But he did have an old stockwhip, in the trunk – where this gun belonged. Finally, he looked at Bell, just man to man, just standing there, and he nodded: 'Yeah. Righto.'

He walked back to the house alone, and went on through the kitchen to the sitting room, where the trunk was – the only thing in the room except that fancy lamp hanging from the ceiling, with its cobwebs and its dust. He'd never been much bothered by the look of a place or lack of material comforts, but it occurred to him now that there was no comfort here at all. He should get a sofa or something; but if he did, that'd only provide another place for the rats to nest. He should get a dog, then, he thought, to deal with the rats, and somewhere wrapped around this idea came a layer of peace, against the crashing of all else.

Yeah, I'll get a dog, he nodded as he opened up the trunk. He didn't know it yet to think it clearly, but he'd been too fearful of letting anyone near since Moz's death – man or animal. It wasn't just the all-day, every-day nightmare of his leaving that was keeping Snow in his own limbo of living death – it was Moz himself. They hadn't been just mates; they'd been much more than that. War forges bonds that no man could ever speak of – not these men, at least, and not in those days. Then, it only brought shame; a shame that burned through every nerve, through every tight-held touch of love. Snow McGlynn would never love again. But he could get a dog. And a sofa, maybe.

He found his old stockwhip in the trunk, kangaroo hide coiled up in a figure-of-eight knot, and tucked behind the boxes of bullets he kept there. Fourteen boxes of bullets, he counted, and he stared at them a moment. What was he doing with all that ammunition? He couldn't remember buying half that much – a box here and there, just in case – but here it was: a stockpile from a war that had ended almost three years ago to the day, but hadn't ended yet for Snow. He lay his gun down in the trunk and, this time, he locked it.

Back out on the verandah, he unfurled the whip and gave her a crack; it had been quite some time since he'd done that, a year or more, since he'd walked away from the farm, and from any communication with his family. Probably time he wrote to his mother, and his brother, let them know he was going all right, when he found the words. He cracked the whip again at the air and, Christ, he almost laughed: stupid thing to be doing, but it felt in some way celebratory, like the marking of something – something good. He walked back over to the trees by the wharf and got right into it, cracking away, striding up and down. And he did let go a laugh when he looked up and saw that it seemed to be working: after ten minutes or so, the birds couldn't settle. He kept going at it as the sky began to bruise through indigo with the dusk and the flock rose as one again – he could barely believe it, but there they went, buggering off.

When he looked back down at the river, all softly glowing in the fading light, he saw Jack Bell down on the bank beside the wharf. He was holding up a couple of cod fish; he said: 'Care to join me?'

Every word Snow owned flew back down into his chest; he couldn't say a thing, but he nodded: *Yes*.

And there they sat together, saying nothing and not needing to, while the fish cooked on Jack Bell's fire at the water's edge. Snow looked up into the trees, to see if the birds had returned, but all he saw was the Southern Cross, its five bright stars pulsing, four large, one small, all dancing, exploding in their own lonely silence, under the boughs at his back.

*

It was an expensive evening. When next Snow rode into Bourke some days later, and there made his application for the employment of Jack Bell, he received a fine of ten pounds, six shillings and three pence. How the magistrate arrived at that precise figure, Snow would never know, but supposed he'd earned an added extra for swearing obscenities at an officer of the law, as he had done to that Sergeant Brandell – the little piece of shit.

The constable who took his money didn't mention it, asking only for the form: 'What work are you getting the blackfeller to do?'

Snow refrained from telling him where to shove his paperwork; he replied: 'What I tell him to.'

'Yeah, ay.' The constable grinned – like the little piece of shit he was too.

And Snow ignored it, signing on the line; he hadn't seen Jack since that night by the river. In the light of the campfire he'd seen the regimental patch on the shoulder of his coat, though, folded on the ground between them: a rectangle split on the diagonal, he couldn't see the colours to determine the regiment precisely, but it was Light Horse. There might have been a time, not long ago, that Snow would have instantly presumed such a coat had been stolen by such a man. Not this time, not this man. They'd spoken only of how good the land was looking with the rain and the gentle flood of winter just past; how sweet the cod was, too; only a handful of words, but somehow Snow knew: Jack Bell had been over there with the rest of them, though he'd guessed most likely in Palestine. Snow had never been the smartest kid at school, but he was a decent thinker, he could nut things through. He could join the dots. And he could decide of his own accord that it was very fucken wrong that this man was tramping, all alone, and hiding from the police.

He'd be offering Jack Bell whatever work he had going – and he'd be getting him to pay off that ten-pound fine through it. He was feeling generous, but not that generous. The first lot of labouring he'd have going was getting in some grapefruit: he was so pleased with the way his oranges and lemons were coming on, he thought he'd take advantage of this incredibly good growing weather and go early with his grapefruit plans. Grapefruits were also becoming increasingly popular at breakfast tables across Sydney and Brisbane, and he didn't want to fail to capitalise on this by being too strict with his own schedule of plantings. He wanted to get in before the prices on small trees went through the roof, as they were tipped to – and there was his further business in Bourke that day.

He left his horse at the trough outside the courthouse and walked down Oxley Street, the main street of town, to call in at the labour agent, seeing if he could get that odd bloke Ross Brock, who'd been with the gang that brought him his first lot of trees, to bring this next lot out from the railway. Two big pubs, each one big as the courthouse, sat almost facing each other either side of the road here, and they were both full of shearers: one favoured by locals, and one by blow-ins, all glancing for a fight. Could have been any spring-time wool town in Australia, except this was Bourke, where drinking and brawling were the main recreational activities. And none of Snow McGlynn's business. He touched the brim of his hat as he walked on; he'd never understand why it was that no one ever gave him trouble, why no one his whole life had ever picked a fight with him, that he carried about him an air of serious-bastard that was intimidating at ten paces, and had been since he was a boy – never mind what soldiering had done to him. He just thought people didn't like him, and that's why they glanced away. But then, none of us ever really know ourselves, do we?

The labour agent bloke recognised him straight off, jumping up from his desk: 'Mr McGlynn, what can we do for you?'

'I'm looking to see if a truck can bring another load of trees out – I'm after that feller by the name of Brock,' he said.

'Him in particular?' the labour agent asked, scratching his bald head at the strangely specific request.

'Yes, him.' Snow wanted to do the man a favour, if he could. It had come to him since his awakening from his own dire despair that there were plenty worse off, and Brock was one of them: his Soldier Settlement acres in Nyngan weren't worth the paper their transfer-of-title was written on, he remembered Stu telling him; and the last newspaper Snow had read himself, a week ago, had told him too many returned men were facing ruin – unable to work their soil, unable to stock their bare paddocks, unable to pay their debts. It was a disgrace: to sell a man land he had no chance of making any money off, unless he has a spare few hundred pounds to make improvements – money none of them had, because they'd just given up five years and the best of themselves getting wrecked for their country, and for no obviously good reason. 'Yes,' he told the labour agent, making it doubly clear: 'I want that feller Brock to bring the load – that feller with the little kid.'

The agent nodded: 'All right, I'll see what I can do. You know it ain't his truck, don't you? And I think he's shearing at the moment – dunno where.

Tell you the truth, I'm not sure he's still on the books. You know he lives down Nyngan way, don't you? He's not really from round here.'

Snow almost said, 'Don't worry then, get someone else,' but something stopped him. He saw a picture in his mind of that little snowy-haired boy digging with his little-boy spade in the dust, and without thinking on it further, he told the agent: 'I'll wait to find out. Let me know when I come back in next week.'

The agent shrugged: 'You're the boss.'

Snow touched his hat in thanks and left.

A tawny dog eyed him from across the street, as he returned along it for his horse. He hardly noticed that dog, though – it was the same shade of dirt as the road.

GRACE

The storms dried up as summer arrived in Sunshine, the air quickly set to crisp bake, the meadow grasses parched to palest gold, and the west horizon was permanently blurred in the uprush of every last drop of moisture from the land. That is, except wherever irrigation pipes were laid. Patches and stripes of wildly vivid green clashed against the red earth, so that every time Grace Lovelee looked out of her kitchen window onto her garden she just about shouted: 'Christmas!'

And every time she reaffirmed her decision, too, that there was no chance in hell that she'd be putting on a turkey for the day itself, or lighting a fire of any sort. As it was, with two days left until Christmas, she was lighting the copper in the laundry for one last wash of sheets and other essentials. The truly wonderful thing about this heat, though, was that

the sheets dried almost as soon as they were hung –
and the smell, the sweet, toasty smell of fresh linen
on the bed, well, she'd never known anything like
it. Such a delight, it was, to slide into those sheets
of evening; they were in need of further laundering
almost daily, too, as she beckoned her husband to
join her.

Oh! Her breasts seemed to swell at the very
thought of him: if he were here in the laundry
with her, instead of being down at the nursery with
Jack Bell, playing with his sprinkler system, she'd
want him again right now. They'd been enjoying so
much of each other, she wondered if he was edging
towards *that* mood – Naughty Boy – an insatiable
want of sexual ecstasy that was almost always a prel-
ude to a crash. As she scrubbed at their pillowcases
now, she attempted to promise herself to try to calm
things down, to somehow steer his desires into more
tranquil waters, but she didn't know how. It seemed
she couldn't say no to him any more than he could
to her; perhaps they were held to each other in some
kind of folie à deux.

'Are we both mad?' she asked the soap, rhetor-
ically, because she knew the answer to that. She
thought she might have known the answer of an-
swers to her increased appetite for Art, too, and the

actual enlargement of her breasts, but she daren't let her wishes botch it up should it be true this time. And that all only brought a flush of guilt and fear: should she be letting him inside her at all if a child now lived there?

She reached across to the tap above the concrete sink, to splash her face with cold water, but the water in the tap was already tepid, though it was only about seven o'clock, and she shouldn't be wasting the tank water on such nonsense anyway. Of course it was unlikely they'd run out of water altogether, being so close to the river, but she didn't fancy the prospect of the taps running dry, of having to pump water from the depths of the Darling, and boil it before every sip.

Another strange fear hurtled through her: what *was* she doing here? This place, so alien to her, and she such an alien in it: the thought struck her seldom, but when it did, it struck hard. What would her parents make of her circumstances today? Their idea of faraway was Paris, where they'd honeymooned thirty years ago and hadn't returned since. They'd barely ever left the South of England – they'd never needed to, so ensconced were they in the middle of the middle class there. Her mother had never even stood at a copper before, doing her own washing.

Australia, her mother had sighed, all concern and scarce belief as they'd said goodbye at the ship, as if she and Art were headed for some place of dragons and sea monsters that lay beyond the Peloponnese. *The things we do for love*, Mother had clicked her tongue, reaching into her pocket for her handkerchief.

It wasn't only love that had brought Grace here, though, was it; it was war. She had washed worse than her own stained sheets; there were the general drudgeries of nursing, of course, things about being human we'd all rather not know about, but there was one boy, a boy from Lancashire, who couldn't have been more than seventeen or eighteen, whose eyes she had to wash of chlorine, from an attack of poison gas – from the green cloud, from the devil's very breath that swept across Flanders Fields. That boy's scream was one of the most chilling she'd ever heard and ever would: a tortured rasp as the chemical had burned his lungs and throat; he died several long hours later. *Must get these cases irrigated quicker*, said the medical officer in charge of that casualty station, as though it were any ordinary occurrence. That's what war does: it changes one's understanding of normal, and it can never be changed back again.

The deepest and darkest fear scored her: had it

all made her somehow infertile? Were her feelings of fullness, her guesses at pregnancy merely phantoms of wanting which would never be fulfilled? She was almost twenty-nine – was she getting too old now to conceive?

At that moment, some angel of mischief sent her a sign to shake her from these grim meanderings: a great groan, like the sound of giant farting, erupted outside the laundry door. She leant across to see: a camel. An enormous camel. In her garden.

And – 'Oh dear Lord!' – it was munching into her tomatoes. Munching into her vine-ripened plans for Christmas dinner.

'Shoo!' She ran out into the morning, brandishing her washing prod. 'Shoo! Go away!'

The camel only kept on chewing, unperturbed, nosing through the thick leafy stalks for the juiciest ones, pushing over the stakes as it went.

'Stop it!' Grace gave it a whack on the side, but to no avail.

'Bleuuurrrggkkk,' it only spat, glaring at her sideways, barely, as if to say: 'You go away – can't you see I'm busy?'

Can't you see I want to make a tray of stuffed tomatoes? With a filling of smoked ham and rice. 'Oh please.' She could only stand there with her hands on her hips and watch – until it had satisfied itself and, with another forceful groan, slowly loped away, down towards the river, no doubt to cleanse its palate.

'Well . . .' Grace looked over the damage: it wasn't too bad, really – only one stake collapsed and ravaged. And then she realised the camel might not be going to drink at the river at all – but might be on its way to Art's young rockmelons and honeydew.

'No!' She ran across the yard shouting. Art was so happy with the progress of his melons, all planted out in a little quarter-acre patch, all flowering – she couldn't bear the thought of his disappointment should they be trampled and gobbled before they could fruit. The melons were fenced, of course, but oh the fence was too low to keep out a camel. 'No!'

She needn't have worried, though, for there was Jack, expertly clapping at the animal, warding it off and then chasing it away, his own strides loping and sure, before walking back to Art. She watched the two men talking for a while, under the colonnade where the young citrus were to go, when they arrived, sometime today, so it was hoped. Theirs was such an easy relationship, she could have watched them all day, one passing a length of iron pipe to the other. Easy, except that poor Jack seemed to have the rough end of everything. He still camped on the river, said that was his home and his choice, but Grace wasn't so sure about that. He said he was happy: he was diddling the system earning above-rates wages from both Art and that 'cranky-arsed McGlynn' but only claiming the latter so the Protection Board of Aborigines couldn't withhold all his money. Grace tried to imagine what it might be like to have the government automatically confiscate your pay; but she couldn't imagine that life. Jack Bell needed McGlynn's permission just to go into town – or risk arrest. The man was a prisoner as it was – and why? Only because he was an Aborigine: classified as fauna. An animal – actually. Wildlife. Try as she might, Grace could not see how any adult, educated human being could consider this a reasonable state of affairs. Not even the Welsh, at home, were treated with such contempt – and most certainly not of a kind enshrined within acts of parliament.

Art had told her: 'You have to understand, it's all very sensitive – the tribes are dying out, all their ancestral lands have been taken up, and the government doesn't want a fuss about any of it.'

A fuss, I'll say, thought Grace, not understanding much of this at all, but knowing that if she walked in Jack Bell's shoes, in his bare feet, she'd be inclined to make something of a fuss about it. She knew enough to realise, though, that whatever she might say, someone might listen to it, and that this wasn't the case for Jack. Even still, she had that queasy, sinking feeling, that if she wrote any letter on his behalf, it would be a letter that mysteriously got lost – like the letters she'd written to the British Medical Association during the war, expressing concern at the absence of demonstrative compassion shown to patients suffering nervous shock. What would she know? She was just a nurse, just one woman, rescuer of hundreds, put the kettle on. But for all she didn't know, it sounded to her that, in this instance, the government wanted things on the hush-hush – why else would you want to lock away unarmed and largely unlettered people? What had Australia really done to them?

To Jack.

How she wanted to do something for him, something meaningful and immediate, something useful, but she just didn't know what that might be. He wouldn't even come into their house for a meal. Whether it was that he preferred to keep his own company, or that he didn't want to be beholden to a boss he could never fully trust, she couldn't possibly know; perhaps it was only the load of his hurt, too heavy and too wide to fit through the door.

Perhaps the redgums at the river were what he needed more than anything else at this time. They were shouting love and life and Christmas in a pageant all their own, and she smiled looking at them now, their broad sprawling canopies framing Jack and Art and all their work. Their flowers were extraordinarily gorgeous: dainty sprays of white fringing, each thread tipped with gold, fanning around lime centres shaped like elves' caps. From this distance they made the trees appear frosted, as though they'd had a little overnight snow.

She walked that feather-headed notion back around towards the laundry, to finish her washing, and as she did, she bent to pick up what she thought was a stray piece of ribbon from one of her pairs of knickers, fallen on the ground: she'd thought it was a little decorative bow come loose, a little blue bow. But it was a daisy, a little blue daisy, sitting in a sparse and thirsty-looking clump of grass. She crouched down to peer at it: a baby-blue wheel, so stark, so fabulous, here upon the rich red timeless soil; and such a surprise: she reminded herself all joy was surprising, never coming as dreamed or planned.

The little bloom brought to mind a poem, a whisper of long ago, and not so long ago, when Germans weren't enemies but merely annoyingly competitive cousins – a tiny poem by Goethe they'd been required to translate at school. It had been about such a small bright flower, which the poet resisted plucking for its beauty; instead, he scooped it up roots and all and transplanted it into his own garden to bloom evermore. *Must I be picked to die?* she'd struggled over the flower's plea to remain unpicked; and here it was again fluttering on the periphery of her memory like the outstretched tip of Death's black wing.

Stop it, she stared for a sliver of a second into its featureless dead black face, before she snatched it from her vision and trod it into the ground: *You will go away.*

She sang it away as she kept on for the laundry: 'When will you pay me? say the bells of Old Bailey. When I grow rich, say the bells of Shoreditch . . .'

Back inside the little tin-walled outbuilding, steamy dim with the copper now boiled, she went straight to the cupboard for her soap flakes, to add them to the water, but after groping around in the depths, she couldn't find them. 'Oh, Art . . .' she immediately supposed he'd pinched them for some genius scheme. She thought she'd have one last grope about before cursing him, though, and as she did, her fingertips brushed the top of what might have been a box, shoved right to the back. Grasping it, she knew it wasn't a box: it was a book. Out it came with a puff of peach-pink, powdery dust. So different the dust was here, she noted for the umpteenth time, so clean-smelling, compared to the mildewy mustiness of English dust. And so much of it – always gathering in places it seemed impossible dust should be, too, like the very depths of drawers and cupboards. It completely covered the leather-bound volume in her hand. She brushed it off the front cover, wondering what book it might be, imagining she would find *Gulliver's Travels* or *Robinson Crusoe*, but she found no title on it, nor on the spine. What a pretty shade of violet the leather was stained, she thought, giving a sweeping touch to the faded gilt embossing of scrolls and fleur-de-lis that bordered the cover, before she opened it, to see, in generously looping script, that this was:

The Journal of Miss Zelma Katherine Bell
1889

Bell?

Grace looked into the pink motes swirling and glistening on the steam, as if they held an answer or a glimpse of the very mystery of life itself.

She turned the page, and perhaps they did:

I might yet be only sixteen years of age, but I have many things to say. My world is seemingly small, out here at Kiriella, with the ratio of sheep to men being somewhere near one million to one, but I see the forces that shape the whole world — all of them — right here in this house.

These thoughts I must write in secret, for if I should be found out as their author, certain forces would cut off my hands and tear out my tongue so that I might never speak of them by any means.

The main force I refer to shall appear in these pages as 'The Master'. We all know who he is — Lord of my Realm and possibly the worst reaches of Hell, too.

I hate him.

I hate him.

I hate him.

He fills me with such confusion he has me believing my thoughts are those that are evil. He robs me of my words and I must fight him for them — fight him here in these pages as I can

nowhere else. I shall write it all down, write it
into the light, for in light there is

Grace turned the page, but there was nothing
there. She turned and turned the pages throughout:
nothing and nothing and nothing. Fear prickled:
had this girl been found out? Had she been forced
to hide this book before it was even begun? And
then not been able to retrieve it, perhaps. Or had
she more simply bored herself with her own ado-
lescent hyperbole? How frustratingly intriguing the
pieces we leave behind can be, Grace thought. Men
with little to say fill up whole libraries with their
words, and this young woman with worlds to say
is afforded barely one page in a laundry cupboard.
There's the lie of history, isn't it. Was Zelma Bell a
fearful yet defiant wife? A cruelly abused daughter?
A highborn debutante fallen to the position of scul-
lery maid, outcast to outback sheep station? Grace
would never know.

She flicked through the pages one more time,
though, thinking how strange and strangely beautiful it is that we are able to affect one another with
such wonderings so quickly and fully, when out of
the back cover slid a photograph: another image of
the homestead, Kiriella, this house, but standing

out the front of it were two young women, one wearing the fashionable tight waist and high collar of last century's end, and the other in plainer dress, working clothes, almost certainly a servant, and a native one, so said her dark skin. They seemed about the same age, and there was something lovely about their pairing, as though they were about to wave at the photographer. Grace turned the picture over, hoping for a note on the back, and there was:

Zelma (me) and Alice

No date, but it must have been around the same time as the journal, judging by those clothes.

How curious . . .

Bell . . .

Was there somehow a connection between this Zelma Bell, Jack Bell and Alice?

Grace felt the weight of a million words unwritten and unsaid in her question.

And then she heard the truck honk its horn up the road.

Their oranges and lemons were here; McGlynn's grapefruits, too.

She had better get this washing done in a hurry now; it would be a busy afternoon.

FRUIT

FRUIT

JACK

When he saw the little white-haired feller jump down from the cabin of the truck, Jack's heart hit the ground with a thud. Nothing unusual in that, these days; every time he saw a bloke with a kid, it'd crush him.

'Don't mind Gordie,' the driver was saying to Art Lovelee. 'He's no trouble.'

Jack could only stand there like he was stuck to the spot, his mouth gone dry and his mind gone off somewhere else as the driver explained to Art that the boy was without his mother and it was too close to Christmas for him to want to be without the boy himself. The driver nodded as he passed by Jack, on his way round to the back of the truck to begin unloading; it was a pleasant sort of nod, but still, Jack couldn't move.

He looked at the river through the overhanging

boughs of the trees, a small boy himself once more. His mother always brought him out here, if ever they got away from the parsonage at Bourke; they'd sit there under those trees, quietly; his mother could sit for hours saying not much at all, looking at the water; grateful for the silence, she'd say; 'Be quiet,' she'd click her tongue, if ever he chattered and badgered with all his questions too much. He'd sit there by her all those hours, playing in the dirt, making soldiers out of sticks and stones, and hoping a boat would come along to break up the quiet. Back in those days, riverboats still ran up and down, churning up the water with their great paddle-wheels, stacked high with bales of wool; a band might be playing on the upper deck if it was carrying wealthy passengers; one summer, the water was so low, one of those boats got stuck ten yards off from the old wharf at Copeland's Corner, so it was called then: McGlynn's place now. Jack couldn't say what year it was that boat got stranded there, that's how little he was, but the company that owned it went broke and left the vessel there, decaying, like the wharf itself. Not a splinter of it left to say so, though, and Jack felt like he was no more there himself.

'You right, Jack?' Art Lovelee was beside him,

concerned; a good man, for all that his mind hopped about from one thing to another like a willie wagtail on cocaine; he was always concerned; kind. He could feel the eyes of the driver on him still, too. He could have been back in the army in that moment; just one of three blokes about to unload a truck. No such distinction as black or white but yes sir and no sir, get on with the friggen job. Why did it have to take the insanity of war to make things so equal and reasonable as that? Stupid friggen question.

Jack looked down at his bare feet with the return of disgust he felt for his own weakness, his nothingness. He glanced back up at Art and said: 'No. Not too good today.' He walked away, not knowing what to say or how to say it – there was just too much going on. Too many emotions, so that he hardly knew what he felt. Too many thoughts, so that he didn't know what he might think.

Art Lovelee seemed to understand, in his way, and let him be.

Jack walked down along the river strand, past his camp where the tea tin stuffed and rattling with his money was buried in the side of the bank. He had a lot of money in there now: almost fifty pounds, it was, and not just what he'd been earning lately, but all he'd had left from his deferred army pay as well. He'd almost paid off that ten he owed to McGlynn, too – that bloke was mean with a penny, meaner than a flea's arsehole, but he was going to the trouble of under-reporting his wages to the Board, so that Jack could get more in his pocket, on the principle of the matter: 'What is this country coming to,' McGlynn had spat, 'taking a man's wages like that? Fucken Bolsheviks.' What Jack was going to do with all his cash, he had no idea. He couldn't lob into town and spend it all on beer – he'd likely only get the shit kicked out of him for darkening the doorstop anyway. If he kept saving it up, he'd soon have enough for a place of his own, a little house on half an acre on the outskirts of town, but what for when the neighbours there would only object to a blackfeller living next door? He was sure the police wouldn't allow it somehow anyway. He'd never heard of any Aborigine owning a house – like it must have been against the laws of nature.

He looked upriver, Brewarrina way, and a thought flashed into his head as though it might have been an answer: go to the station there: do something there: get the mob behind you: *change* things.

I can't change *anything*, he told the river sand.

'Jack! Jack!' It might have been a corella laughing down at him from the trees, but it was Grace calling out to him. Lovely Grace Lovelee. She was standing on the top of the bank, waving at him; something in her hand.

He gave her half a wave back, but still he couldn't speak.

'Jack, I've found something that might interest you.'

He tried to look interested as he took the few steps up the bank towards her: 'Yeah?'

'Yeah.' She smiled, making yeah sound like it belonged to her; Jesus, she was good-looking. She held out a photograph: 'It might just be a coincidence, but it's an intriguing one. This woman,' she pointed to one of the women in the picture, the white woman, 'her name is Zelma Bell. Have you ever heard of her?'

'No.' He shook his head, but he kept staring at the black woman, recognising her almost straight-away. The photograph wasn't clear enough to show the features of her face in sharp detail, but her stance, her hair, the way she held her hands in front of her – he'd have known this woman anywhere.

'Jack, what is it?' Grace asked him; concerned, too; so kind.

And he said, tears of a lost child in his eyes, every lost child: 'This woman.' He touched her face in the photograph: 'This woman is my mother.'

SNOW

Bloody unreliable. Snow had nothing against blacks, really, and never would, but how can you respect a man who doesn't show up when he's supposed to? When he's agreed he would. *Not like I've been hard on him*, Snow said to himself, perplexed; he thought he'd been fair; he thought they'd been getting along well; he was annoyed, too, because Jack was that good at any work, you never had to tell him what he needed to do. He was doubly annoyed that the dog at his side would not stop barking – had not shut up since the truck had started coming along the track. This dog had followed him home from Bourke the trip in before last, that way things just happen soon after you think them – as though he'd called the dog into his life. This dog didn't know what she was – part kelpie, part several kinds of terrier, part old scrubbing brush – as nameless as she was breedless, and apparently his.

'Shut up!' he yelled at her.

She shut up, but her tail wagged madly, slapping against his knee, as he walked over to meet the truck.

He said to Ross Brock at the window: 'You want some extra work? I could do with a spare pair getting the trees in and watered before the end of the day.'

The man nodded, fewer words in him than Snow had himself. The little kid stood up on the seat, hand on his father's shoulder, and wordless, too. They both looked at him with clear blue-grey eyes.

Time stretched along the gold lines thrown by the westering sun; the dog panted; a blowfly hummed slowly somewhere near; and after half a small eternity, Ross Brock asked: 'Where do you want 'em?' Meaning the trees; where did he want the truck pulled up for easiest carting.

Snow pointed past the rows of lemons: 'Just the other side of the orchard there.'

The truck trundled up the rutted track and stopped where the new rows had been prepared for the grapefruit. When Snow joined Ross Brock at the back of the truck, he heard the little boy say, 'Can I get a drink, Dad, please?'

Such a little boy, not much more than a baby, really, no taller than the dog, and talking to his father with such manly respect, Snow looked at Brock with a deeper regard: his was a tough hand, but he was doing a remarkable job with that kid.

Brock said to his boy: 'You take the water bottle down to the river and fill it up. Don't muck about there or you'll fall in and drown.'

Snow wasn't all that impressed with this idea, thinking the boy was too little for the task, but he didn't say anything: *Not my kid to bother about.* He got stuck into the work and didn't give it another thought, except for the drift of something sad in a rarely visited corner of his mind, that he'd probably never have a family of his own. He didn't really want one – he didn't want the complications, the woman, or the worry – but it was still sad. *You sad bag of shit,* he lugged the first of the trees into the farthest hole and shovelled it well in.

They were fine-looking trees, bigger than he'd been expecting and undamaged by the oven-hot journey; he was pleased with them. His only concern was the reach of his irrigation; the oranges and lemons furthest from the pump were not quite getting their fill as it was, and although they were healthy enough, they were obviously smaller; not by much, but enough to keep Snow awake at night wondering how he'd fix it.

He'd not paid any more attention to Brock but for seeing the trees go in, and they were over halfway through the work when he saw the man's shadow, long and rangy in the deepening afternoon, meet the shape of his own.

'Yeah, mate,' said Brock. 'Ah. Lost sight of Gordie. Sorry.'

And he was off, tall legs down the trench-row for the river.

That'd be right, was Snow's first thought. *I do not need this going on here.*

But he pulled himself up as quickly and followed the other man, boot print on boot print, down the soft, damp mud, until he was running too. The bloody dog was nowhere to be seen either, and something about that gave Snow a shiver: *Fuck.*

'Gordie!' Brock called for his son, and Snow's whole chest cracked in two for the man; this was what the world was coming to: a man, trying his hardest, and losing.

Losing.

Losing.

'Gordie!'

Losing everything.

'Gordie!'

Down at the corner, above the wharf, they

separated, Brock running west, Snow east towards the Lovelees' place.

'Gordie!' Snow could hear Brock calling and calling, and the desperation in the man's voice sharpened all of Snow's senses, searching for the kid: in every ripple of the Darling, so slow at its surface, but full of snags and grasping eddies below. A duck feather caught in a patch of reeds; an old bootlace washed onto the gravelly sand; a bleached twist of driftwood crept up from the depths like a skeleton hand.

'Gordie!' Snow was calling for the boy now, too, panic jangling in his knees. 'Gordie!'

'What is it?' That Lovelee bloke was running down the bank by the old schoolhouse towards him: 'What's happened?'

'The boy! The boy!' Snow shouted at him, the first words he'd had for this man. 'The Brock boy – he's wandered off.'

'Which direction?' Lovelee asked, snapping to; and they recognised each other in that life-and-death snap: two men who'd never met before, but who knew what to do.

'Dunno,' said Snow. 'Brock's gone Bourke-ward beyond the wharf, along the river. I'll carry on this way.'

'Right,' said Lovelee. 'I'll search the scrub beyond the track, back of your place.'

'Right.' Snow didn't glance behind him to see the man go, his focus returned fully to finding the boy. 'Cooee!' He sent up the call and it rang round the sky. 'Cooee!' He wasn't calling so much to the boy but to anyone who might be nearby or on the north side of the river, where there was naught but uncleared gidgee and ferals: goats, pigs, camels. And snakes everywhere: king browns, red-bellies, copperheads. 'Cooee!'

It brought Jack Bell out from wherever he'd been skiving, appearing from the thick scrub that sat between river and track at the southern boundary of the Lovelees': 'What's going on?'

'Little kid's wandered off,' Snow told him, not wasting words now: 'Three years old or thereabouts, little white-haired boy, gone about half an hour ago.'

Jack nodded: 'I know the kid you mean. I'll double-back.' And off he went, second-checking the stretch of river where Snow had just been.

'Cooee!'

The sun fell and fell to the cries of the men.

And all the birds were silent, as though they waited, listening.

GRACE

She'd thought it was another knock at the door, but it was only a beetle hitting the bedroom window. Christmas beetles, they were called: glossy bronze with an iridescent sheen to the wings and almost the size of a penny, they would make for attractive baubles, if she'd bothered with a tree – and if the creatures hadn't been so terminally stupid.

Clunk – one beetle was followed by another, and another, and another. *Clunk, clunk, clunk, clunk, clunk, clunk, clunk, clunk, clunk, clunk, clunk, clunk.*

A small plague of Christmas beetles hitting all of the front windows of the house.

'Why?' she asked them. Unlike moths, who were obviously attracted to the light, these beetles didn't seem to need a reason to smack themselves senseless against glass or timber – so that they lay all about the front verandah like drunks, legs swimming in the air. Such an awful sight – pathetic and vaguely macabre – she'd taken to sweeping them off as soon as she heard them, which had been three evenings in a row now. 'Their season doesn't last long,' Art had promised her, and she'd heard that certain trace of sorrow in his tone as he'd added: 'I used to collect them, every year, when I was a boy – boxes of them.' And she'd asked him: 'Whatever did you do with boxes of them?' Couldn't help herself, and he'd said: 'Oh, I'd just look at them. I didn't understand then – you know.' She did: he didn't understand then that they were dead. More reason to sweep them up so he didn't have to look at them.

By the time she'd retrieved her broom to do just that, the beetle storm had abated, leaving perhaps twenty or so scattered on the boards, some upturned, some crawling slowly, painfully, as though disoriented, some quite still. Grace looked across the yard, wondering again what brought them: perhaps a trick of the light: she looked back again at her windows, reflecting the lilac blush of the gathering sunset; perhaps they simply thought the windows were the sky; or perhaps something else, altogether imperceptible, caused them to fly at the house. *Too sad*, she sighed for those at her feet: these beetles that all looked the same on the surface, like boys in uniform, but were really each their own creature, and she swept them gently.

It was only then that she became aware of a ruckus overhead – the welcome swallows swooping about, gurgling urgently, as though an actual storm might arrive any moment, although there would not be a speck of rain at all this evening. She looked up: they seemed to be darting around the nest, swirling about it, as if something was wrong. The baby birds had emerged from their eggs perhaps a week ago – she wasn't sure, as the rafter was too high to really see, but a week it was since she'd seen the first little flame-coloured beak appear above the rim of their twiggy snug – one, then two, then three, and maybe four. So wonderful, so alien – what did she know of their ways?

Then through the greying gloom she saw it: something fluttering fitfully, fretfully, something which did indeed seem very wrong. One of the babies was at the side of the nest – flapping its wings desperately – upside down, its tiny foot caught among the twigs.

'Oh dear – no!'

She rushed inside, into the bedroom, to get a chair, her own heart beating to match the baby bird's distress. She wasn't sure what she wanted more: to save the bird, or to save Art from witnessing its too-dreadful demise. He'd be walking up the path to the house any moment, she was sure. *Quick*, she urged herself up onto the chair: *Quick!* Even on the chair, she had to rise up on her toes to reach, and in that reaching the swallows swooped and swirled more and more urgently. Her hand trembled so terribly at this small crisis she wondered how she was ever a nurse, and as she found and grasped the tiny twig-leg between her thumb and forefinger, warm feathers thrumming against the heel of her hand, she was sure she'd hurt the poor thing worse than its predicament ever could – as if she'd never before hurt someone to make it better.

The birds, so close, now cried around her head – *PLEASE! PLEASE! PLEASE!* – their arrow-wings swishing past her ears, roaring over a call that shouted: *COOEE! COOEE! COOEE!*

'Oh God save us all!'

But at last, she managed to unhook those needle-tip claws. The baby bird struggled then in her palm, writhing, petrified, and she almost dropped it, before she tipped it, rather roughly, back into the nest.

She stood on the chair with her hands pressed together and her fingertips pressed to her lips in the prayer: *Please, be all right, baby bird.*

Baby.

Baby.

Baby.

And then in that prayer she heard: 'Mrs Lovelee! Grace! Grace!'

A man – not Art, obviously. A heavy gait, lumbering fast, and thick fair hair fairer against the darkening sky. It was their neighbour, Joseph McGlynn. Snow McGlynn, so Jack had told her he was more commonly called. Snow: how oddly endearing Australian nicknames were, she thought, even as she saw the fear now written on his face. The gruffer the man, the sweeter the moniker, it seemed: Bluey; Froggy; Noisy Ackerman; those she'd nursed slipped through her mind, burly Australians with nursery-rhyme names. And here was Mr Bitter Misanthropist, Snow McGlynn, but with such a fear in his bearing, somehow fearful in his whole being, she stepped down from the chair but she didn't hear what he said to her next.

All the fears and the songs within her sang silent around and down into her stalwart verse: *When will you pay me? say the bells of Old Bailey. When I grow rich, say the bells of Shoreditch. Pray when will that be, please? say the bright bells of Stepney. I am sure I don't know, says the great bell of Bow.*

Don't tell me, don't tell me.

I don't want to know.

Behind Snow McGlynn, she saw a grey shadow-shape bouncing towards the colonnades: a kangaroo, unmistakably – and finally – a kangaroo. She didn't care now if that creature or any creature ate the entire planting out of melons. She thought: *This has been an interesting day for animals. I don't want another interesting thing to happen.*

Lord. It's Art, isn't it. He's done it, hasn't he. He's gone.

He's left me.

He's dead.

'Grace?' Snow McGlynn was asking her; pleading with her: 'Mrs Lovelee? Have you seen him? He's about three years old – Ross Brock's son. With the truck – the trees.'

'What?' Grace could barely pull herself away from that worst of worst, the sweep of that great black wing obliviating all.

'The boy – have you seen him?' Snow McGlynn was catching his breath, leaning on the verandah step, looking up at her.

She frowned, willing herself to return to the reality at hand: the boy.

'Oh yes. Of course,' she said to Snow McGlynn: 'Little Gordie – the driver's boy – he's here, in the kitchen.'

She'd quite forgotten him in the run of events these past few moments: he'd appeared at the back door, in company with a shaggy brown dog, both of them asking for a drink of water; she'd filled the bucket for the dog, and as she'd just made lemonade for Art, from the warty but wondrously tangy lemons on the old squat bush at the back of the privy, she'd sat the boy down with a glass of that and a bowl of grapes; she'd asked him: 'Does your daddy know you've come here?' He'd shrugged: 'Daddy is busy.' She'd been going to walk him up to McGlynn's as soon as he was finished his lemonade, but then the beetles – *Oh, what's wrong with me!* It was not like her to be so scatterbrained, so distracted, not like her at all.

'He's here?' Snow McGlynn appeared relieved and disbelieving at once. He took off his hat and wiped his brow with a sleeve, as the dog came skittering around from the back verandah, head down, eyes pleading upwards at him, expecting some chastisement, but receiving only a vague pat on the head.

'Yes, little Gordie is here.' Grace beckoned Snow inside, the dog too, and down the central hall they went, her smile curling around her suspicions confirmed; her hand on her belly: yes, it was true, she *knew*, she *knew*: she held a baby there. This would surely explain her eccentric behaviour of late – well, *this* eccentric behaviour, at least. A tell-tale sign she'd seen in a few of her junior nurses who'd let love fly in the face of war: a plumpness round the hips and an overbusy emptiness in the head – and then straight on a ship back home.

As she walked towards the kitchen she felt a change in her step, a low-slung satisfaction; she felt her muscles let go and relax; she felt the elastic in the soft silk of her knickers stretch against her swelling belly. She felt each touch of heel and toe upon the floorboards press the foundations of the house more firmly into the soil. She felt her future, all futures, truly settling at last.

'Your father is going to tan your hide,' Snow McGlynn said beside her in the kitchen and the boy blinked up at him from his place at the table, terrified, small hands either side of the bowl, its contents plucked entirely of grapes: this boy had been hungry, too.

'No one's hide will be tanned or otherwise

harmed,' Grace dropped her voice an octave, the way a woman must in giving orders to a man.

'Right.' McGlynn gave her a curt nod and left – with the dog, his dog, it seemed – hobnails and paw-nails clipping the fresh linoleum on their way out the back door.

'I was bad,' the little boy said into the bowl, far too sombrely for a boy so small.

Grace pulled out the kitchen chair opposite him and sat down. 'How old are you? Do you know?'

'Free,' he said, not looking up; ashamed. 'I am free.' Three, he meant, counting out three little fingers – and bless.

'You're a very grown-up young man for only three,' she said, her heart aching for him.

'I was playing with the nice dog,' he said, confessing his crimes. 'I lost Daddy's water bottle. I don't know where it is. I looked and I looked, but I don't know where it is. I don't know where I put it.'

Oh my heartbreaker.

'I'm sure your daddy is more concerned for you than any water bottle,' she offered.

But the boy shook his head: 'I went off with the dog.'

She resisted telling him there are far worse things a young man can do. And thank God for dogs – this one was probably looking after him, bringing him to safety, with that peculiarly caring sense dogs so often have. Bringing him here, perhaps. A last blast of sun filled the window behind the boy's dear little head, turning his straw-blond hair bright gold; dust motes turned to glitter, floating in the air between them, and something more deeply beautiful tingled through Grace, as though raspberry sherbet ran in her veins.

The little boy changed the subject. 'My birfday is in Nobember,' he said, still not looking up.

'November, is it?' Grace was amazed, and not only at the child's conversational skills. Such an intelligent little boy – Art had trouble remembering the months of the year and he was thirty-seven.

Outside, Snow McGlynn was calling to the others; the dog barking along: 'Found him! Cooee! Found him! Cooee!' That cooee call she'd thought, when distant, had come from the swallows, and now came with a great clanging sound, charging up the hall – startling her and the boy both. It took her a second to work out that McGlynn was ringing the dinner bell that swung from the front verandah awning there – an iron triangle that had come with the house but which she hadn't thought to use as yet. McGlynn was determined to wake the dead with it.

She said to the boy, assuring him once more: 'Don't worry. Everything will be all right, I'm sure.' And she got up to light the lamps, in the kitchen, and in the hall. She didn't really know anything about this little boy, whom she'd only met briefly, down by the colonnades – barely a 'How do you do' – she'd been too intent on finding Jack, to show him the photograph. 'This woman is my mother,' Jack had said, holding the picture before him, falling into it. He'd then walked away, and she'd felt awful at that, as though she'd handed him some fresh deed of pain; she resolved to try to talk to him about it later, and returned to the house then, to get her washing in, before any blustery dust could spoil her sheets. Returning to the kitchen now, she looked at the little boy here anew: he was motherless, too.

And she would not let anyone tan his precious hide.

'Gordie!' Stomping across the verandah, the sound of the flyscreen door almost wrenched off its hinges.

Grace stood between the rage and the boy, all the firmer for the abuse to her flyscreen, so lovingly restored.

But the man who crashed through her home now crashed with screaming, searing love. 'Gordie?'

He quietened his voice on seeing her, searching her face: 'He's here?'

Such sadness in that face of his: a young face, too lean and lined with care; eyes so very sad, she had to force herself to hold their gaze: she saw in them all she needed to know of his tragedy. She stepped aside: 'He's here.'

'Mate,' he stood over his tiny son, words jagedged and plain: 'Don't you ever go off like that again.'

The tall man and the small boy looked into each other a moment then with every unspoken thing.

There was the story of Australian men, Grace brushed away a happy-ending tear, and as all other boots clomped into her kitchen, with the smell of salt-sweat and grimy thirst, she said: 'I suppose you'd all prefer a beer to lemonade?'

'There's a good idea,' said Art, already reaching into his trouser pocket for the bottle opener, flicking it out from the penknife casing with a thumb. 'You'll stay for one, won't you, Jack?' he said over his shoulder.

For Jack Bell was in their home at last.

*

Well, isn't this Christmas, Grace thought to herself,

all her wishes come true, listening to the four men discussing sprinkler irrigation in the lounge. The most glorious sound in the world.

She heard Art get up, declaring, a little drunk, 'We need some music, don't we what?'

She heard the crank of the gramophone winder and the trombone beat start up: 'I gotta brand new sweetie, better than the one before . . .' A recent favourite, Jolson. And soon Art was bellowing the chorus: 'Does she go, "La-da-da-da, I don't care"? I'll say she does!'

'Getting rowdy in there, isn't it,' she said to little Gordie, who was standing on the chair beside her at the stove.

He was intent on watching her stir the pudding custard; she'd just told him it was a dull job, having to be careful at it for ten minutes or it'd burn or go lumpy and be ruined, and he was taking his watch-duty very seriously.

She asked him: 'And what are your favourite things to do, Gordie? What do you like to play?'

'I like rocks,' he told the custard.

'Just rocks?' Grace tried not to laugh, but she couldn't keep the laughter from her voice: he was too adorable.

'No,' he told her, looking across at her, such a

grave little cherub: 'I like cake, too.'

'That's handy, isn't it.' She nodded at the plum pudding just boiled and steaming on its plate; she'd made it weeks ago, for Christmas Day, but it was fitting that they should share it tonight, since they were all here and so together.

Little Gordie beamed with the shared conspiracy: 'Yum.'

Yum, indeed.

But plans are only dares for disappointment, aren't they?

'We'd best get going.' Ross Brock was at the kitchen door half a second later, hat in hand.

'Oh, but you must stay for pudding,' Grace insisted. 'It's Christmas – well, it's Christmas in Sunshine, at least.'

'We're expected elsewhere,' Brock said, somehow defensively; sharply: 'It's late.'

'Oh. I see,' said Grace – not really seeing at all, except that it was wrong of her to presume they might not have had any particular place to go. Or perhaps he just didn't approve of jazz or Jolson. Still, she wouldn't have the little boy disappointed at the loss of cake. She hastily cut a slab and placed it in a bowl, smothering it in custard before giving it to Gordie: 'There you are.'

'Thanks all the same,' said the father, 'but we should go. Got to get the truck back to town and meet the last train home, to Nyngan.' He had the boy by the arm, half pulling him off the chair, taking the bowl from him, too.

'Take it with you, darling heart,' she said, gently pushing the bowl back into the boy's hands, his silent, observant face unreadable. *No wonder you ran away from Daddy.* What was this scarred and hardened generation doing to the next? She gave the boy a spoon for his pudding as well and told him: 'Can't have you going without when you did such a good job on that custard.'

He looked up at his father, unsure.

'Can't take your things with us, Mrs Lovelee.' The father was a stubbornly humourless chap.

And so Grace matched him sentiment for sentiment: 'It's a bowl and a spoon, Mr Brock. We do have others.'

'Right.' The man nodded; then tapped the boy on the shoulder: 'Say thank you.'

'Thank you,' said the boy, and they were on their way, the headlamps of the truck golden eyes in the night and gone too soon.

She waved once at the black and stepped back past the lounge room.

'I'm a *jaaaazzz* vampire!' Art had put another record on the gramophone. 'Shake a foot, shake a foot and *daaaance* with me . . .' He was quite drunk now.

Ain't we got fun, Grace quickened her step up the hall, the quicker to get pudding into him; it had been such a long day. She yawned as she prepared the food on a tray, waiting for the kettle to boil. She yawned and yawned. She might have enjoyed a gin right now, but she was curiously off the booze: maybe that was baby choosing its preferences too. Was it a him or a her? My, my and la-da-da-da, how much she did not care either way.

'Yeah, I gotta get going, too,' she heard Jack say in the hall.

'Wait!' she called out, pouring the water into the pot. 'Tea's made!'

But here was Jack now in the doorway: 'Sorry, Grace. Time I called it a day.'

'Oh?' She wanted to protest, but it was enough he'd stayed a while as it was, so she only said, 'See you, then,' and felt oddly Australian with it; or rather awkwardly Australian: you needed the accent for authenticity: *see-ya*, exhaled as one word along a breath without moving the mouth.

Jack stood there a moment longer than 'see you',

though, as if he might be about to say something else. But he only patted his shirt pocket, where she could just see the top of the photograph she'd given him, or returned to him, and he said, 'Yeah. See you.'

He closed the flyscreen softly behind him and she followed down the hall with the tray – just as Snow McGlynn stepped out: 'On my way, too, Mrs – Grace.' And he smiled – a smile from him was an extraordinary thing in itself, but this was a smile of such warmth, he seemed a different man. A returned man, perhaps.

'Goodnight, then.' She smiled back, a little indulgently, victoriously. But she added, almost having forgotten: 'What are you doing Christmas Day? We'd love to —'

'Going home – tomorrow, to Condobolin. Going to surprise me mum.'

'Oh!' She wasn't sure why, but that seemed the sweetest victory of all. 'Safe travels,' she said: 'And Merry Christmas, Snow.'

'Merry Christmas to you, too, Grace.'

'Cheerio!' She smiled him out the door.

And now here was her Art, lazing back, feet up on the arm of the sofa, Heifetz's violin zinging like a lovesick mosquito round Chopin's Nocturne in E Flat.

'Christ, I thought they'd never go,' he said, sleepy eyes suddenly alive: not very drunk at all.

She laughed: 'How I adore you.'

'Put that tray down, woman, and come here.' He pretended Dancing Dawg; yes, he was just pretending; reclining; wry.

She said, practising her Australian accent, tight-jaw, loose heart: 'I'm not keen to risk it.'

'Risk? Me?' He made himself the joke: 'But I'm such a sure bet, such a dead cert.'

A half-moon sat in the window, aglow, as though it were looking down on them from a dress circle seat in the diamond-splashed sky.

She said: 'I'm serious. I wasn't going to tell you until Christmas Day, but I . . .' Her blood fizzed with more than love, more than life; she touched the place their child called home, for now: 'This ain't too much shortbread, love. You know how I said I wasn't going to bake anything this year?'

'What?' He sat up smartly, gripping his knees, on the edge of his seat. Oh, how wonderful he was.

'Yes,' she said. 'How's that for Christmas?'

'Christmas?' He was crying, unashamed, weary and beery tears streaming, taking her in his arms for the best dance, the best embrace, there ever is: 'Really?'

'Yes.' She matched him tear for tear: 'A bit of peace on earth, a bit of magic, just for us. Hm?'

He shook his head: 'No. No magic to it. All good things happen because of you.'

HARVEST

HARVEST

JACK

He left for Brewarrina straightaway, hoping to be there Christmas Day – when there'd be less chance of any trouble from the police at his arrival. He knew Snow McGlynn wouldn't make any formal objection to him leaving; he'd just think that's what blackfellers do, go walkabout or whatever.

Jack wasn't entirely sure what it was he was doing, except that it was better than doing nothing – and doing it on his own. He needed help. More help than the Lovelees, lovely as they were, could ever provide. If he was going to find his daughter, if he was going to find himself, he needed some strength of numbers to even begin to face the challenge. He needed other blackfellers, just like him.

If he stayed at Sunshine, he'd only be perpetuating his mother's life, and his grandmother before that: living on his own land but at what cost? What pain was it that kept his mother from telling him she was raised right there at Kiriella? He'd never know. That's what that photograph meant most to him: the raggedy black woman and her white-boss friend, they look happy enough smiling for the camera, but they're not really friends. Friends are equal – man to man, spirit to spirit, dust to dust, in every law.

Equality: that was something not so much worth fighting for as a fight he could no longer ignore.

He had money in his pocket, enough to start something. Start along this path, wherever it might lead. The Seven Sisters would guide him, through this night and all nights to come, as they always had, his mother with him every step.

Jack Bell walked and walked towards the rising sun, a sun that touched his face like loving hands and shimmered up the Darling, all over this land: his home, in every leaf, every feather, every grain of sand.

He was ready to take it back.

SNOW

Snow McGlynn couldn't look at a corella without thinking of Jack Bell, and since Jack's technique for upsetting their daily roost worked so well, he didn't see too many anymore. He often wondered where Jack went, missing the silence of his company, his easy competence at any task. He probably missed him in ways he couldn't speak of, if he let his mind go there – and he didn't.

His mind stayed mostly with his trees, and it paid off quicker than he'd ever imagined it might. His first saleable crop of the Eureka lemons came at the end of January, 1922 – and not only were they unexpectedly abundant, they were lip-smackingly beautiful. The following year, he got seventeen tons of lemons in all; eight tons of oranges; five tons of grapefruit – and paid off just over half his development advance. He was doing extremely well, luck falling his way on every count: that year saw the whole district struggling in drought, but thanks to the overhead sprinkler system Art Lovelee set up for him, his citrus was not only viable but sold at a premium.

The year after that, 1924, he bought all his new stock from the Lovelees' nursery – fine young trees they were. They had quite an operation going together, Snow and Art; with the Kiriella melons, plums, apricots and strawberries fetching decent prices as well, they combined resources and invested in a cooling system for Snow's packing shed. Art purchased a truck they could share, too, to get their cases of produce up to the rail – it had 'SUNSHINE FRUIT CO-OP' painted in bright orange lettering up the side. Art would make him drive it, and laugh at him getting up in the cab, calling him a communist every time. Snow didn't mind. They were forging an industry there in fruit that would quietly blossom and grow for decades to come, and they both knew it.

Even still, it wasn't until almost Christmas 1925 that Snow got around to changing the front gate on his property so that it no longer said 'Copeland's Corner', whoever those Copelands might have been. It wasn't until then, with his loans paid off, that the place was really his. But he didn't put his name on the gate; he just called it 'The Corner', as it was generally known anyway; nothing and no place would ever seem his enough for him to want to put his name on it. He finally bought a sofa, though, and a good couple of beds for the spare room, for when his mum came up for a visit, sometimes his sister and her kids as well.

There were times, for sure, now and again, that he felt the absence of a family of his own. But then his old mate Stu Egan would bring along his – having married a nice girl from Condo and settled not far from there at Yarrabandai. They had three kids already, and Jesus, were they brats – spoiled as. Stu couldn't tell them no for anything. The two elder ones'd tear up the rows, making a mess, whingeing and crying and carrying on. But Stu was so happy, Snow didn't mind too much.

He fixed up the old wharf of its broken timbers and rusty nails, so all the kids could play down there. And Snow could chuck them off it, into the river, for a bit of fun; chuck the old dog off after them.

When he was alone, and it was a bit too quiet in the night, he'd think about Moz. But it was all right, now. Mostly.

GRACE

'**M**umma!' Grace clasped her daughter's hand to cross the road, for the post office. Such a small town, Bourke, but today it seemed as frantic as pre-Christmas Piccadilly Circus – or perhaps Grace really had left behind all trace of pressed-together Englishness now, changing her perception of what constituted a crowd. The street here was wide and sandy, a strip of desert complete with stray camel parked in the centre of it, oblivious to pedestrian and motor traffic alike.

'Mumma! Pick me up!' Her daughter, Eliora, was three and a half and too big to carry – or too big in Grace's state of advanced pregnancy. The baby wasn't due for a month yet, but she was huge this time: too heavy and too hot. *I'm not doing this again*, she promised herself with the novelty of all this warm weather having well and truly worn off.

'Mumma! Sore *feet!*' the child began to wail.

Grace dragged her along: 'Sore feet? You don't know the meaning of sore feet, Ellie.'

'Yes, I do!' Her daughter sulked: 'You're mean, Mumma.'

'Mean?' Grace laughed. 'You don't know the meaning of the word mean, either, Ellie.'

'I do!' The little girl dragged down with equal force on her mother's hand.

Dear Lord, Grace sighed. What was the child going to be like at fifteen when her wilfulness was highest? 'Eliora Lovelee?' Her mother-in-law had peered into the bassinette at first inspection of the baby: 'What is she, a lolly?' Too sweet, and how she was: the prettiest picture-book child with a halo of gold curls and great big blinking-thinking blue eyes. Now she was a little pain in the arse. *Not true*, Grace scolded herself, and then scolded Art and whoever invented the rule that children can't accompany men anywhere unless it involves playing some sort of ball game or the purchase of ice-cream. He was only at the labour hire, seeing about getting in a gang of fruit pickers for the Christmas strawberries and stone fruit, while Grace was picking up her catalogue order from Foy's department store, in the city – complete delivery of yuletide, from tinsel to toy tea set, from bonbons to new maternity brassiere – half a dozen parcels, for which she'd need both hands.

'Be a good girl, darling, and we'll go and have a chocolate milkshake when we're finished . . .' Oooh, yes – they'd have one of them anyway. The chocolate milkshakes at the American Candy Shop Café were the reason she had her mail delivered to Bourke, rather than the one-horse outpost that was North Bourke, nearer Sunshine. Like mother, like daughter, Ellie smartened up at the promise of chocolate anything and without further ado they entered the blessed cool of the tall, grand portico of the Post & Telegraph. Outlandishly grand, it always seemed, this building, with its two-foot-thick iron lace trimmings and chequered marble floor, a monument to days gone by when the wool trade made this town five times its present size, before drought and flood and flood and drought again, and cattle baron Sir Sidney Kidman more recently buying up all the small holdings he could get his hands on, any Soldier Settlements gone bust and any Crown land further outback that might have been left to the full-blood, tribal blacks. 'Won't stop till it's all a wasteland,' so Art would say at any mention, of the quiet war that sets greed upon nature, one that never seems to make the front page of any paper.

'Mrs Lovelee, good morning.' There, at the central counter, was Mr O'Reilly, the assistant postmaster with half a smile for her beneath his black eyepatch from whatever screaming piece of military metal smashed that side of his face. He turned and called over his shoulder to one of the postboys sweeping the floor up the back, snapping a finger at him: 'Barlow – take Mrs Lovelee's parcels out to her car. There they are.'

'Thank you, Mr O'Reilly – that's very kind.' Grace was very grateful.

'More necessary than kind, I think.' He chuckled softly at her burden of babes, reaching over the counter with a bull's eye peppermint for Ellie.

'Say thank you,' said Grace, and her heart clenched every time she gave her daughter this ordinary instruction, her thoughts winging back to little Gordie Brock, for the grapevine chat through the labour agency that told her his mother had taken her own life, drowned herself, not long after he was born. She'd been a nurse, at a repatriation hospital, one who married an angry, wounded soldier; no need for further gossip. Originally from this very town, her name had been Caroline Forrest, before she married, a name that rang a bell somehow, a faint bell. But they all did, didn't they?

'Thank you.' Ellie blinked up at the eyepatch man with her big baby blues, and took the peppermint, even though she didn't like it.

Good girl.

'Now, I'm sure there's some letter mail come in for you as well,' Mr O'Reilly said. 'I'll check, save you going around to the box.' He left them to do just that, and she was grateful for this kindness, too – their post office box was below knee level, somewhat inconvenient for those barely capable of crouching or bending, and she just remembered Art had the key. Never mind, here was Mr O'Reilly, coming back, a couple of envelopes with him: 'There you are.'

'Thank you.' She glanced at them as she took them from him: the one on top was a receipt upon payment from one of their seed suppliers, she knew without opening it; but the other, addressed in handwriting she didn't recognise, looked somehow important, its small, neat block lettering somehow personal; she flipped it over and saw the return: *J. BELL*, and a street in Redfern, Sydney.

Jack.

She knew it was him immediately, wherever he was, and she tore the envelope open there and then.

Dear Grace,

It has been a while. I think of you and Art often, but I have not had much to say until now. I am in Sydney these days, working at the Eveleigh Railyards.

When I left your place that night, I went out to Brewarrina, thinking I should be with my own people. It is a sorry place, full of too many who have had too much taken away. There are no real jobs and no hope for the children being raised there. There is only servitude and little or no pay.

Some other men and I decided to try our luck in the city. Redfern is a place now where a black man can work as any other man, labouring with the railways, chopping sleepers with a broad-axe, or sometimes carting produce up to the markets, doing the heavy work whitefellers don't want to do, so we were able to get permission to go without too much trouble. Whenever I see the name 'Sunshine Fruit Co-Op' stamped on a crate I smile, knowing it's you there.

It has been the best decision, me coming to Sydney. Last year I met a man called Fred

Maynard who has begun a movement called the Australian Aboriginal Progressive Association. He is an inspiration to me and many others here as well, a black man speaking out with force and fine language on matters of equality in the law, the right to vote, to have opportunities for education, and fair wages. We are a political organisation, and thanks to the efforts of our Secretary, Mrs Elizabeth McKenzie-Hatton, who has travelled the state all year with our message for justice and fairness, we have now grown to eleven branches and five hundred members.

Elizabeth is a few years older than you, but you share the same spirit. She is trying to help me find my daughter, Mary. We haven't had any luck with this as yet. The Queensland Aboriginal Protection Board is less helpful even than the Board in New South Wales. But we will keep trying. I will find my little girl one day.

In the meantime, I have begun to study the law myself. I am not permitted to enrol at any college or university, but that doesn't prevent me from educating myself. It's a long road, but I'm on it.

Anyway, I wanted you to know that your goodness towards me has come to some good. I

hope to see you again when I return to Bourke,
with the AAPA – possibly next year.

With respect and great fondness,

Jack

'Mumma!' Ellie was dragging on her hem now. 'Let me see! What is it? Let me see!'

Grace showed her: 'It's a letter from a friend.'

Ellie scrunched up her nose: 'I can't see.'

'You will one day,' Grace promised her.

'What see?' Ellie asked her, doubtful and scowly and possibly about to scream for that milkshake.

Grace promised her a good deal more than that: 'Sunshine, darling.' She smiled for all good things, touching the top of her daughter's sweet head with the letter, gold curls brushed and blessed with Jack's words. 'It's just a little sunshine on a page.'

AUTHOR NOTE

Sunshine is a fictional place, an imagined hamlet outside the town of Bourke, in far north-western New South Wales, on the edge of Australia's red desert centre. Everything that happens in the story happened in this country, though.

The Soldiers Settlement Plan, devised by commonwealth and state governments during and after World War I, was a great idea at the time, and while there were some successes, like that enjoyed by Grace and Art Lovelee, and Snow McGlynn, by the mid-1920s it was clear that the scheme had been a failure, as it had been for those like Ross Brock, who were sold unworkable land. It was certainly another devastating blow to those Aboriginal people moved off their country to make way for it, but their experiences weren't officially recorded.

Similarly, the experiences of Aboriginal soldiers

during that war were not recorded, and their contribution to the Light Horse regiments in Palestine, in particular, has until recently been ignored. It's impossible to know how many Aboriginal soldiers served, with estimates ranging from five hundred to a thousand, but it's beyond doubt that the country they returned to shunned them. Men came home to find themselves homeless, unemployable and, in some instances, their children 'removed' by the various state Aboriginal Protection Boards. Jack Bell's situation was tragically too true, for some.

But Jack's resilience is also inspired by the real-life founder of the Australian Aboriginal Progressive Association, Charles Frederick Maynard; he wasn't a soldier, but he was the first Aboriginal political activist to organise mass protest and gather the intellectual power of Aboriginal people for justice in a formal sense. 'I wish to make it perfectly clear on behalf of our people,' he wrote to Premier Jack Lang in 1927, 'that we accept no condition of inferiority.' He laid the foundations for the fight for Aboriginal self-determination and equality, which continues today, and it's astonishing to me that he's not a household name.

Fred Maynard was helped by the indefatigable white activist, Elizabeth McKenzie-Hatton, who had begun her social work as an Evangelical Christian church missionary but whose understanding of and advocacy for the plight of Aboriginal people routinely brought her into conflict with the church and the Aboriginal Protection Board. Fred and Elizabeth are shining examples of what can be achieved together when love and justice are placed at the centre of action.

For the curious, the Goethe poem referred to by Grace on p.79 is 'Gefunden' ('Found'). Some readers might also recognise the small boy, Gordie, as Gordon Brock from the earlier novel, *This Red Earth*. And as always, the National Library of Australia's vast database of newspapers, journals and photographs has been an invaluable resource for both historical fact and the flavour of the times.

Gratitude is an inadequate word for the thanks I owe my editor, Alexandra Nahlous, not only for her ever soulful insights and word-wrangling, but for her belief in the importance of Australian stories. To the greatest champion of Australian voices ever, Selwa Anthony, your love for this story sends it out into the world with the best magic there is. And big sunshiny thanks to my publishers at Booktopia, David Henley and Franscois McHardy, for this beautiful Brio edition.

Sunshine is my bittersweet tribute to the spirit of togetherness and understanding that really does sit at the heart of Australia – if only we'd let it shine a little brighter, and for everyone. And above all this is my love song to that glorious blue sky, red dirt country where my muse de bloke, Deano, my own darling husband, was born.

About the Author

Kim Kelly is the author of eleven novels, including the acclaimed *Wild Chicory* and bestselling *The Blue Mile*. With distinctive warmth and lyrical charm, her stories explore Australia, its history, politics and people. Her work has gained shortlistings in The Hope Prize and Australia's premier short novel award, Viva la Novella.

A long-time book editor and sometime reviewer, Kim is a dedicated narrative addict and lover of true love. In fact, she takes love so seriously she once donated a kidney to her husband to prove it, and also to save his life.

Originally from Sydney, today Kim lives in central New South Wales, on Wiradjuri country, with her muse de bloke, two cats and some chickens, and occasionally the kids when they come home to graze.